A Different City

A Different City

Tanith Lee

IMMANION
PRESS
Stafford England

A Different City
By Tanith Lee
© 2015

Cover by Danielle Lainton & Storm Constantine from an idea and photograph by Tanith Lee
Interior illustrations by Tanith Lee: Leafless Tree page 10, Chess Piece page 84, Portrait of an Unknown Actress page 122, After Thought page 184.
Illustration on page 121 adapted from a photograph by Tanith Lee.
Interior layout by Storm Constantine

Set in Palatino Linotype

ISBN 978-1-907737-65-7

IP0120

New (future) Author Web Site, as the original has been stolen:
http://www.tanith-lee.com

An Immanion Press Edition
http://www.immanion–press.com
info@immanion–press.com

Books by Tanith Lee

A Selection from her 93 titles

The Birthgrave Trilogy (The Birthgrave; Vazkor, son of Vazkor, Quest for the White Witch)
The Vis Trilogy (The Storm Lord; Anackire; The White Serpent)
The Flat Earth Opus (Night's Master; Death's Master; Delusion's Master; Delirium's Mistress; Night's Sorceries)
Don't Bite the Sun
Drinking Sapphire Wine
The Paradys Quartet (The Book of the Damned; The Book of the Beast; The Book of the Dead; The Book of the Mad)
The Venus Quartet (Faces Under Water; Saint Fire; A Bed of Earth; Venus Preserved)
Sung in Shadow
A Heroine of the World
The Scarabae Blood Opera (Dark Dance; Personal Darkness; Darkness, I)
The Blood of Roses
When the Lights Go Out
Heart-Beast
Elephantasm
Reigning Cats and Dogs
The Unicorn Trilogy (Black Unicorn; Gold Unicorn; Red Unicorn)
The Claidi Journals (Law of the Wolf Tower; Wolf Star Rise, Queen of the Wolves, Wolf Wing)
The Piratica Novels (Piratica 1; Piratica 2; Piratica 3)
The Silver Metal Lover
Metallic Love
The Gods Are Thirsty

Collections

Nightshades
Dreams of Dark and Light
Red As Blood – Tales From the Sisters Grimmer
Tamastara, or the Indian Nights
The Gorgon
Tempting the Gods
Hunting the Shadows
Sounds and Furies

Also Published by Immanion Press

The Colouring Book Series
Greyglass
To Indigo
L'Amber
Killing Violets
Ivoria
Cruel Pink
Turquoiselle

Ghosteria Volume 1: The Stories
Ghosteria Volume 2: The Novel: Zircons May Be Mistaken

Contents

A Different City
Introduction

It will be obvious to anyone familiar with my writing that large, historical or parallel-historical cities often feature in it, virtually as characters. They have their own personalities and life-force, from Koramvis, the conqueror's capital in *The Storm Lord*, to Bar-Ibithni in the second part of *Shadowfire*, Kol Kataar and Ru Karismi in the ice-locked world of the *Lionwolf* trilogy, the European Paradys (France), Venus (Italy), Petragrava (Russia) and even including Druhim Varashta, the underground city of the demons of the *Flat Earth Series*. These metropoli tend simply to arrive. They have flavours of other 'real' places, known or not, but stay their own creatures.

In that way, like the rest, Marcheval appeared. To me it was a smoky sibling of Marseilles, with a wide, ship-dock land and estuary that I haven't – yet – had space to explore. But as almost all cities do, it has its rivers (or waters), its grander buildings, slums, sinks and secrets.

It is both sinister and beautiful. Never really fully revealed, though often glimpsed, like rare beasts that flit and slip from shadow to shadow, stranger elements are liable to spring out finally, a lightning strike.

There is definitely some all-pervasive demonism present in Marcheval, like an old religion left behind in pieces among the stones. It takes varied forms, yet has a penchant for the sky as a canvas. The fearsome portholes in its fabric offer glimpses of Hell. Or... Heaven?

Ancient cities, and buildings, incline one to a sense, if only for a deniable second, some hint of such a past, or sidelong world, strong and urgent as the concrete present. Time and place show folds in the fabric of their curtains. If you have the courage or foolishness to pull the cloth aside, what will they let you see? When looking in... or out.

The first story, *Not Stopping at Heaven*, has its own strange family history – mine, being based closely on a TV play by my father, (from an unused script from the 1970s). (See the end note of the story.)

It has the brightly barren contrast of a fruitless spring and depthless winter.

The second story, *Idoll*, came from a general idea suggested by an editor friend. The anthology did come out, but by then with a different Lee tale in it. This is an example of the Legend of the Secret Room. And also of the shape behind the mask, which may be a lit lamp, or a vandal's torch.

The last and third story touches on the nature of mortally-hurt love. Now and then, to destroy an adversary is not the indulgence of revenge, but the only fastidious course: *The Portrait in Gray*.

Tanith Lee
February, 2015

Not Stopping at Heaven

For most of us, though not all, there are times in our lives when it seems we have spent some hours, or even days or months, in Heaven. But more often we only glimpse that wonderful place through the windows of a speeding train - a train that does not ever stop there.

Camille St France
From *Post-Revolutionary Reflections*

ACT ONE

Scene 1

How many marriages had the Avenue of Aviaries seen?

Perhaps enough that now the pitted stone pillars and the strange rusted cages that lined it did not bother to take much notice. The occasional tall poles of dusty summer trees looked indifferent – while the birds, that had in the morning flown up with wing-clapping and calling as the two carriages passed, failed to rise for this one coming back on its own.

The new bride was somehow dimly aware of all that, even through the enhancement of her happiness.

Poor old street, Lucide thought to herself. *It would take an explosion to wake it up. Even my tulip gown won't do it now.*

But *he* liked her gown. Of course he did. Guillaume, her husband.

Guillaume Milait. And I am Madame Milait.

She glanced at him, and saw that he looked hot and sulky. (Almost as red as the crimson roses she still carried in her lace-gloved hand.) Too much wine at luncheon. Well, he would have a prosperously solid home life now, a loving wife to care for him. He would settle like a wild bird, and grow calm.

Even sulky and flushed he was, in his tawny blondness, very handsome. They must all have been jealous, but in a nice way, not wishing her any harm - or only Grete, perhaps. No, Lucide would not think about Grete now.

The carriage came to a stop.

As they got out, her husband assisting her, (as she had asked him to), if in a rather awkward fashion, the driver spared no attention. Hired beforehand and paid, he set the horses trotting in less than a second. Off the carriage went, with her feet barely on the ground, and more dust powdered up into the air.

Lucide hoped her gown was not smudged. It was such a lovely rejoicing golden yellow – Summer Tulip, that was the shade of the cloth.

When they were inside she would examine herself again in the pier glass. She had been too nervous, too excited earlier properly to assess how she looked. But she had been at her best.

Today she had appeared young. And Gui had looked older, more mature. This had made nothing of the ten years difference in their ages, nothing of the fact that she, at thirty-eight, was the elder. What did that matter? He loved her. And she – oh truly, she loved him. Her Gui. Her darling.

Evening shadows were already creeping through the house. But it was not quite time for the girl to light the lamps.

Guillaume stood in the doorway, watching his wife as she studied her reflection.

His expression was brooding, perhaps even contemptuous? Surely not. They had known each other only a few months, and been married less than seven hours. More than anything Guillaume seemed as if he should not be there at all, just outside Lucide's private parlour. He was shifty and misplaced. But then, as most of them knew, he had been dragged up in a slum near the Butchers' Quay, not born of the well-off shopkeeper stock that had formed Lucide and her brother.

"I love this gown," Lucide said. "I love the colour. Don't you think it suits me? Don't you think it's beautiful?"

"I can't see anything wrong with it," said Guillaume.

"Grete said yellow was too young for me, but she's always cruel. Jealous."

"What of?" he languidly asked, raising and lowering his shoulders, as if feeling a sudden weight.

"Oh, Gui! Such a *man* always. She's jealous that I'm with a beautiful boy like *you*. They all are. How not, my handsome darling? Oh, it will all be perfect now. You'll never have another uneasy moment. You'll never regret marrying your Lucide."

Guillaume shrugged. (Perhaps the sudden weight fell off at that.) "Grete – damned bitch. As if I'd ever take notice of *her*."

"No, you never would. But she thinks; I'm only six years older than that Lucide."

"She looks sixteen years older." (Lucide laughed,

pleased either by his spite towards Grete, or by what Lucide took to be his loyalty to herself.) Gui went on, "She looks old enough in fact to be your grandmother. Left to me she'd never have come to the wedding. A civil. ceremony – why'd it need all those hangers-on?"

"She's my brother's wife," said Lucide, now unpinning her yellow hat. " Joséphe wouldn't dare come without her."

"Hang Joséphe, too. And by the way, Luce, I'd prefer you call me *Billy*, like I've told you."

Lucide blinked rapidly for a moment. There had been a sting in his tone. Naturally he normally answered to the given version of his name – Guillaume, Gui – but he had, he maintained, an eighth of English blood on the side of his absconding sailor father. 'Billy' had been his nickname in the rough' byways he had frequented for the past twenty years of his twenty-eight-year-old existence. Not everyone, evidently, would be permitted to use it, but he had early on awarded Lucide the privilege. And constantly she forgot.

"And as for bloody Joséphe," Gui-Billy added, "he made a pig of himself at lunch."

Lucide smiled and said nothing. Gui-Billy had been greedy as well, and not only with the food but the drink. Joséphe was not, as Lucide was not, much of a drinker. But never mind it. Soon Gui would settle, become content, and calm. "Well, we won't see them for a while now, my brother and his horrible Grete."

"Tell me when you expect them to visit you," he said, "and I'll take myself off."

Lucide set her yellow hat, and the red roses she had carried, down on a small table.

Her new husband seemed irritable. Something in her

shrank and wrung its hands – Oh, she must make things all right for him, tonight was their Wedding Night. It must not be spoiled. Forever after she would remember – Blood filled her face, red as the roses, red as wine, redder by far, in fact, than Billy's sullen flush. Yes, why not: she could present him with the bottles she had had brought into the house. It was to be *his* special night too, was it not? The first time he would possess her, the first he would lie beside her, sleep in her arms, hold her –

Lucide turned and opened a dark wood cabinet, on the apron of which, until now, only a slender meagre bottle of liqueur had ever stood.

"Another thing too, Luce," she heard him say, as she began to remove the treasure to reassure and tempt him, "this insane business of Joséphe keeping your money in his charge. You're my wife now. The care of any funds must come to me. I thought you promised me you'd speak to the damned miser about it."

Lucide shut her eyes, her back now to Billy.

"You have to understand, my darling, that our father did that, to protect me, when I was very young. It was after that illness I suffered, when I was scarcely more than an infant. I did explain to you, my dear, several times."

"You're hardly sick now. And you're forty–"

"I am thirty-eight, Gui – Billy. Don't make me older than I–"

"Forty, thirty, fifty – you're old enough to take control of the money. Then you can pass charge of it to me. Then you won't need to worry over it. And nor will I."

"I have never kept you short of any money, not since our engagement. No, never. Have I? Besides, we agreed, you might find some work–"

"Oh, I'll get some work, don't fret. But in my own

way. It's due to a man to find his *own* work. And it has nothing to do with Joséphe holding on to all those francs and livres which are due to *you*."

"I'll speak to him, G – Billy. Very soon. But I could hardly do that today, now could I?"

"See you do, then. Or I'll be angry."

Lucide turned, her eyes overbright as if with tears, or fever, some pain or ailment conjured from the past. And she saw that he hated and despised her emotion and her weakness.

"Billy – don't attack me, not tonight, your tongue's so sharp, and I don't deserve it. And not now, of all times. We're man and wife, Gui. I'll – I'll get the money from Joséphe. Trust me. And look–" holding up one of the bottles, a dully gleaming greenish ghost in the hot half-light, "this will make you happy."

Billy glared, then pushed the glare from his face. He went forward, took the bottle from her, and examined it. "Absinthe. That's better than wine, at least."

From the silver tray on the cabinet apron he took a glass. He pulled the cork out of the bottle with his strong white teeth, and for once she did not exclaim that he should be more careful, as if he, for the sake of God, could ever break a tooth on a cork.

Lucide watched him drink. As she did so she sidled away, and not waiting for the maid, who by now was late, lit the painted lamp on the mantelpiece. A soft butterfly wing of coloured lights opened on the room. Even the bottles ranged for Gui's attention took on an exquisite patina. And the yellow gown, catching in the mirror a tinge of pink and emerald fire, charmed her back to soft expectant joy. It would be all right now. He was nervous and awkward, humiliated by her strident relatives. Poor Gui. And a Wedding Day was a strain for any man. She must be kind. She had sworn to him she would always be kind.

She thought, *I shall be able to wear this gown again, sometimes, when we go to some special place. To the theatre, perhaps, or to dine at a special restaurant...*

But she must have spoken aloud.

He stood there, refilling his glass, staring at her.

"No you won't. Not *that* dress."

"Why not, Billy?"

"It's too bright."

"You said it suited me—"

"Maybe for a wedding. Not for any other time. You'd draw too much attention to yourself. People looking at you – laughing, probably."

"Am I so awful?" she asked him in a stunned, childish voice.

"For God's sake. Don't be melodramatic. It's just not suitable, too bright. Like that bloody lamp you've lit. Isn't it hot enough in this damned house already–?"

She thought, *He's exhausted. Let him rest. Don't be upset. He says the wrong things. He doesn't mean to hurt me. I won't let it make me miserable. No, not tonight.*

"I wish," she murmured quietly, "we could have gone to the sea for a few days. Or up into the hills. A rest, and clean air–"

"There'd be no sense in that," he replied. "You need to oversee your shop. Make those idle girls there work, instead of pilfering. The place never really pays."

"Is the absinthe nice?"

"*Nice.* Anyone can tell you're no drinker. No. But it's drinkable, unlike most of the rubbish served at lunch."

"Well... have another drink. We're celebrating, aren't

we? There's champagne, too–"

And she went towards the door to rouse the maid, or see to things herself.

But Billy stopped her with a quick hard: "*Wait.* Now see, I never said before – but I have to go out."

"What?"

"For an hour or so."

"Tonight..." she said. "You have to go out tonight–"

"I'm not embarking for Africa, you stupid imbecile. One hour. And this is important. It's about a job of work – that so-urgent task you've been constantly nagging me over. Tonight is the only chance I have to see this man – he's important, he could help me."

"But – how can it have to be tonight?"

"That's just the way of things. I'm not arguing with you about it. The decision is mine."

With a swift part lurch, Billy slammed down the bottle and the glass – three times filled, now neatly empty – on the small table where his wife had put her wedding hat and roses. The flowers seemed to skitter from him, and quickly fell one by one on to the floor.

"I'll only be gone an hour," said Billy. "Till later, then."

And from the parlour to the dark of the unlit stair, and down towards the street, and into the settling dusk of the City he went, shutting the door behind him, her lover and husband. Not even a farewell kiss. He had not, in any case, touched her since their civic joining, except when, scowling as if with flustered concentration, he helped her from the carriage.

Lucide stands and listens to the opening and closing of the front door. After a while she goes to where the fallen roses are lying. She picks them up caringly and then moves back to the mirror, and holds the roses against the bodice of the gown.

After a brief interval, still holding the flowers, she too goes down through the house, and finds the maid, Bette, emerging sleepily from the lower floor. Lucide tells the girl that she can go home tonight if she would like. This treat had possibly been in the offing, and the maid is gratified, comes instantly fully awake and brimmed with vitality, and within ten further minutes has left the house. Lucide lights two lamps, and leaves one in the hall. With the other she returns upstairs, this time to the highest floor below the attic. Here is her bedroom, a spacious and quite opulently furnished chamber. Both room and bed are easily large enough to accommodate two persons.

Lucide places her hat in its box inside a broad, polished armoire. Next, filling a tall water glass from the covered jug set ready, she puts the roses into it. She stands this glass on her dressing-table. Then, from a drawer, she brings out an expensive silk peignoir and nightgown. In colour they are a deep alluring turquoise, and trimmed with creamy billows of lace. It is obvious that neither item has ever before been worn. They have also been stored with scented sachets. The perfume, freed, fills the room deliciously.

Lucide goes to the bedroom mirror, and holds the silk and lace against herself, gazing at her reflection, wonderingly.

Then she turns and lays the garments tenderly on the bed.

Crossing to the nearer of the two windows, Lucide looks out, then glances at an old clock above the fireplace.

Suddenly her face breaks into a gargoyle grimace of weeping, but there are no tears, and the grimace lasts less than seven beats of her heart. After which her face slackly relaxes.

She sits down in a small armchair. And waits.

Scene 2

The City went downhill below the Avenue of Aviaries, across a square with shops and a market, at this hour mostly deserted, where peelings and leavings littered and flitted in a slight night breeze.

Beyond, the sloping streets descended into ever tighter and meaner huddles. Then came the stink of soiled water, the black night river and the disreputable docks. Here and there a torch burned on a pole. The modern gas street-lamps of the higher thoroughfares went uncopied here. It might still be 1680, and in some of the bleaker holes, it was.

A few dead things – rats, dogs – rested on cobbles, or dry mud tracks with now and then a bit of stone to step on, or stumble over. Monsieur Milait reached a tavern, *The Piping Clown*, and stamped in for a fourth and fifth absinthe. He would be late for his pre-arranged meeting, but that was *her* fault, Lucide, so why hurry now?

But at length he left the public house and entered a winding alleyway, at the termination of which a thin and dispiriting hovel bulged its upper storey over a wall.

"You took your leisure, Billy," she reprimanded him, as soon as he stepped into the room. "Late, *late*."

"What was I to do? I got here as soon as I could. When did I swear to be early? It was my bloody Wedding Day, Jeanne."

"And what am I. to do? What did you think it was like for me? Waiting and waiting and pacing about here."

"Shut your mouth. I've had enough drivel from the other bitch. One thing you *can* do, fetch me a drink."

She tossed her head of oil-black hair. She had green eyes and a waist narrow as a wooden pen. As unlike mouse-brown Lucide as was conceivable. And eighteen years younger, too.

From a cupboard in the wall she took a jug of Holland Gin, and two chipped glasses off a ledge.

They sat on stools at the plank of wood that served for a table, and in the middle of which burned a sweaty yellowish candle. It was one of twenty she had, this thieving slut, filched from Lucide herself, though over a year before.

"To your health, Monsieur," she mocked him. Then, "Well, get on, if you must – tell me about your *wedding*."

He would, he sluggishly thought, rather have lifted her on to the plank and straddled her. But *women*. They never stopped their noise, their demands and questions. Jeanne Croll fired him up, however, and had done so since first he met her, half a decade before, he then twenty-three and she fifteen. It had been the briefest connection, and presently she was gone. Nor, then, did he care so very much. But last year – he twenty-seven, she nineteen – he had met her again near the Quay of the Vigil. He had been on burglary business, while she was earning a little on the side, as her feckless husband, Antoine, had been sent to a remote prison, with hard labour.

Aside from the whore's trade, she had another job too, in a big old shop by the Aviary Market. The emporium sold groceries and also such commodities as cups and plates, soap and candles, sometimes even good cloth, velvet, silk. From the cornucopia of which slim wicked Jeanne stole, frequently, restrainedly, cannily and undetected. This shop belonged to Lucide.

Now Jeanne waited in her alleyside dilapidation for either Antoine Croll to be released, or – by now – Gui-Billy to sort out her illegitimate life.

"The wedding went the way they do. But she's still done nothing about telling brother Joséphe to let go of her money."

"Didn't I warn you? You *simpleton*. Oh, glare if you want, you know I'm right. And perhaps she's invented all of it – there *is* no money her brother looks after for her. After all, what is she, some mental idiot?"

Tempted to rage and hit her, Billy felt by now too tired. "She says it's got to do with some illness she had when she was a child. And she doesn't lie to *me*. Think. She has that house on the Avenue, that's worth a lot, and the shop, that's all hers – a little goldmine. And Joséphe, blast him to Hell, is surely rich enough – you should have seen the carriage they drove in, him and that evil hag he married, that Grete."

"And you married another hag, just to get hold of her money. But now she won't let you. You've achieved nothing. Aside from the slavery of wedlock."

"One day you'll bite off your own tongue, Jeanne, you vicious cat. Listen, I don't go back on my plan. I'll write to him, that Joséphe. Remind him I'm in charge of her now. Or else I'll find a lawyer."

Jeanne flung back her head and laughed. She threw the last of her drink down her throat and refilled both their glasses.

"I tell you now, my Billy, whatever you do, you need

to work as fast as lightning. We're in *danger*."

"What danger?"

She pulled a face at him, ugly and nearly fearful to him, flaring up as it did, and yet oddly not cancelling her sexual tastiness. He wished he had never met her, he thought. Let alone that old bag, Lucide. His – *wife* – which also in its way, he was sure, was Jeanne's fault.

"*Look*," Jeanne spat at him.

And on to the plank she cast a grubby bit of the cheapest paper which, to Billy's displeasure, he saw carried the stamp of the prison justiciary.

However, even if that was clear, the writing on the paper was not. Though he claimed he could read and write, Billy was not much of a scholar. And besides Antoine Croll was even less of one.

For a minute or so the semi-illiterate Billy peered and puzzled over the scribble of the almost entirely illiterate Croll.

"Oh – in the name of the Virgin!" Jeanne's reprimand came like the crack of a whip. She tore the letter back, and fishing in the pocket of her dress, took out a pair of 'nose-nippers', tiny little spectacles that would clip on the nose. If the two most significant men in her life were dunces, Jeanne who could read and write well enough, was blind to both mediums without ocular help.

She scanned the letter, and read aloud in a scornful, bantering way, "'I shall be comed home in a monith–' he means a *month* – 'and my and thou wull been agin united.' Do you see, Billy Milait? That vile garbage is to be let free early for some unbelievable virtue of conduct – the prison must be mad – and so let loose on me. And once he is, he will *kill* me, Billy. Oh yes. And then, make no mistake, he'll go to look for *you*."

"God – let out of jail – is that what he says? But how can I work that quick with her, with Luce–"

"You have to. Do you want me dead? Or him killing *you*?"

"Why does he have to find out we've been together? We could just keep clear of each other for a while. Until I have the money managed, and then we can get off like we planned–"

"Oh! That would suit you, wouldn't it? Fob me off, and just make do with her, with *having* her, that silly old woman, no need for you to go short!" Jeanne removed her spectacles, as if she had seen enough, and thrust them back into her pocket.

Billy was affronted. "Christ – do you think I'd ever touch her? God knows I could have. She's been on her knees for it from me ever since I met her–"

"And I'm sure you answered her prayers. *You* say not. How could I know?"

"You know *her*. You've worked for her. Do you think I'd go with that?"

"She's not so bad. I've seen worse. She's old, but she's a *woman*, isn't she? Somewhere to stick yourself. That'll do."

"Shut up, you bitch."

"How can I? And what's more, I can't shut up to Antoine, either. If he comes here and I can't get away, I'll have to tell him."

Billy stood, and crashed both his fists on the plank, so the candle dipped and the jug jumped a foot sideways, gin spilling, sparkling.

"I'll fix you so you'll never utter a word."

Jeanne too rose up. She stared straight in his face and said, with a sort of awful, bitter dignity, "I won't be able to hide it, Billy. Even dumb. I'm carrying your child. Your son, I'd think, judging by how he weighs on me already."

"Lies, you lying slut. There's not an extra inch on you."

"I'm slender. But he's *there*. You'll see that soon enough. And so will bloody Antoine when he walks in."

Billy slumped down. "Abort it."

"How loving you are. How caring. Do you think I'd give myself over to these slum doctors? My sister *died* of that. *Never*. I'll carry him and bear him. He's my child too." Abruptly her green eyes, free of the nippers, seemed to shatter into peridot tears. "Oh, Billy – my love – I *want* your child. I love you so. I'll love you till I die – And you. You only want to see me have my insides wrung out, you only want me dead. Well. Once *he* gets here I soon will be. Me and your son. Oh, Billy."

Billy sat and stared at her. Then he poured himself some more of the surviving gin. He said slowly, "I don't know what I can do. I need *time*."

She sobbed, then smothered her sobbing. "Find a way. We don't need all her money, do we? You're strong, and I am, too. We can work, and once the baby's born, well, we might try for another life in some other country. You can make a fortune in some places. Listen. Doesn't the old witch have any other cash, *in the house*? They always do, the wealthy ones. They hoard it. She had a little stash at the grocery shop. I saw her go to it once, by accident – pretended I hadn't seen. But at home, in that house – she'll have something all right. Maybe... *thousands*. In some cupboard, under a loose board – under the mattress even. Where you'll sleep with her."

"Lace up your bloody mouth, Let me *think*."

"Think quick, Billy. Time's in the hour-glass and it's

almost all run out."

"There's still a month."

"There *isn't*, Billy. Less than that. *Ask* her for the money, perhaps, though don't say you know she's got a secret hoard. Say it's to start you in a good job, a partnership, something that will profit her, too."

"That's where she thinks I am tonight, visiting some industrial lordling, who'll employ me."

"And she believed that, did she?"

"Why shouldn't she? She knows nothing about us."

"Oh, women *know* things, you'd be surprised. After all, remember, you called on me when I was working in that grocers. It was just before she threw me out. Said I'd pinched a bag of sugar. Stupid cow, I'd had a hundred things, never *sugar* – far too obvious."

Billy again got up. He walked round the filthy and subsiding room, whose walls were full not only of gin cupboards but holes and cracks. Certain corners stank of rats, living and deceased. Water dripped somewhere, like the river tapping with its ancient fingers: *Let me in.*

"All right, Jeanne, I'll tell you. She *has* a stash of coins and notes, in a chest at the bottom of the clothes closet, in her bedroom."

"The bedroom where you've never been."

"Of course I've been there. But not to do anything with her. She gave me a house key weeks back. Obviously I let myself in now and then, when that maid of hers had gone off. And then I had a look around. I found the money quite soon."

Jeanne had gone white. She leaned toward him as he rambled by and rasped: "*How much*?"

"I never counted it. Hundreds probably."

"And how much have you already robbed her of?"

"Not much, a few sous, or a little more. Enough for a good cigar or a bottle of something. But she won't find out. *She* never counts it. It's curious, she's old, but she's like a child. Besides you and me, Jeanne, she's like a child of ten or so." He added feebly, "But I want more than what she keeps in that chest. God knows, I'd never have married her otherwise."

"No. Forget all that! Things have changed. You'll grab what you *can*. For *me*. For *you*. For our baby. *Him*."

Across the table-plank then he reached out and seized his mistress, this glowing white and peridot icon, with her Hell-forest of black, black hair. He could no longer control the pelting rage in him that was abruptly transposing to lust.

And she was malleable now. "Yes, Billy. *Yes* – whatever you want. Have me – *kill* me, if you like – but don't leave me here for that miserable ape Antoine to murder."

"As if I'd let you die," he said, and pulled her face and her body against his.

As she wound her arms about him she knew she had won the battle. He knew it too.

But even as they writhed across the groaning plank, he vaguely remembered that he was not yet shot of his unattractive, clinging, rich old wife – and that soon he must go home to her.

To their Wedding Night.

Scene 3

By night, or in the earliest pre-dawn morning – the clock from the church above the market had just struck two –

some of them said you could hear the ghosts of the birds, whirring and shifting, flying across the larger cages, or singing, or *talking*, for there had been chatting parrots kept here, as well as song-thrushes, in the Avenue of Aviaries, in the days before the Revolution, and sometimes it seemed their spirits came back to visit. Certainly history itself had recorded that every caged bird had been let free, one Revolutionary evening. Out they had hopped and fluttered, and some took to the skies, mimicking the new Age of Liberty. And some had died too, in those hours, when hawks or other predators, (not excluding man himself), spotted such inexperienced and easy prey. But some birds, confused, or tame, only returned to their perches in the opened cages. So then they were left to make their own way, or to starve. Such was the nature of Liberty, almost a century before.

Now Gui-Billy, as he toiled back up the slope toward Lucide's house on the Avenue, began to think – though not believe – he could hear a faint chitinous and feathery whispering, a rustling on top of some of the pillars or within some of the recesses... and there – *look* – a stream of winged things lifting from a tree to cross the snapped plate of the arid summer moon. Bats, maybe, from the church.

Gui paused. He felt worn out. It had been a stressful day, and he should never have given in to his urge to possess Jeanne. Even going back into *The Piping Clown* afterwards had only briefly revived him. At least, Lucide must surely be asleep by now. She was used to shop hours, rising sometimes before daybreak, sleeping nightly not later than ten, or eleven.

Gui raised his head as a cool breeze passed.

He tried to draw all of it into his hot and weary body.

But it only made him cough.

And then he glimpsed the Fair Lady up there, miles above the Avenue as it sometimes looked, as if the hill it lurked on had stretched itself, and the streets here crouched down. Gui did not like the Cathedral. Sometimes, on the upper walks, he had gone out of his way not to pass it directly. Eccentric really, for he believed he was not afraid of God. Did not even believe in God, except as something handy to blaspheme.

When he tried the key in the lock, for a second he feared she might have bolted the door. And the maid had been sent off, he recalled – to leave them private for their romantic night. Would he get in? But the door obliged him. That was all right then. He had only to get up to her parlour on the second floor and take one more drink. Then he could sleep on the big sofa there. He sighed with relief as he shut the door on the ghostly, fluttery street.

At the sound of a blundering step on the stair, Lucide started awake.

For a moment she did not know where she was, and then, realising she was in her bedroom, and had been sleeping in the arm-chair and fully clothed, she could not understand why.

Was it her Wedding Day today? What a silly thing, see – she had dressed in the special yellow gown – and then – *oh, fool, fool* – fallen asleep and crushed its folds – she would look like a scarecrow and Guillaume would be embarrassed by her.

Then the uncouth footsteps sounded again, downstairs in the house. Who was it? Had someone broken in?

On her feet now, shaking out the folds of her skirt, Lucide half-recollected some dream she had been having.

It was a silvery dream, here and there ribboned through
with soft rose red. She retained no other details, except
for the atmosphere, the sensations she had had while
dreaming it, which were all very strange to her: a type of
headiness, a sort of *anger*, a kind of *arrogance*. None of
them belonged to a waking Lucide. How peculiar it was.

Two things occurred at once. Her eyes fell, in the low
lamplight, on the flowers standing in her water glass.
And simultaneously she heard the unique pop of a cork
in the parlour below.

The dream vanished.

Reality, and real memory, returned.

"Christ on his cross! Are you still up? I thought you'd
have been in bed by now."

So he greeted her, balanced in her private parlour with
the champagne bottle in his hand, from which a spray of
wine had leapt out to spatter the wallpaper and the
carpet.

Although the dream was gone, another anger had
begun in her. It was born solely of pain, and the
frustrated outrage of bewilderment. She had known it
often as a child. This too she did recall.

Billy, scowling, tipped the bottle back between his lips.
Plainly, none of it was meant for her.

Lucide: "You seem as though you don't need any more
to drink tonight." The voice that came from her was harsh
as a crow's.

He gulped his bellyful, lowered the bottle. "Don't you
go telling me what I need. I *need* a bit of bloody peace.
And I'll drink as I like." To reinforce his opinion, he took
another swig. Then, bottle still clutched, he staggered to
the sofa and thumped down on it, so the room seemed to

shake. He had managed to ignite her painted lamp, (causing the dome to sit crookedly), and its lights were careering everywhere from vibration. To him this was like being in a galloping carriage. He did not much care for it.

And she stood there, staring at him with her round colourless eyes. He had never seen her look like that before.

"Don't stand there watching me. Get to bed."

"That is a vintage champagne, Gui. Joséphe sent it. It was meant for both of us to share."

"Go on then, have some," he jeered. "It's not the best I've sampled, but it's drinkable."

She ignored this. She said, "It's gone two in the morning, Gui. You certainly have treated me very beautifully, today, today of all days. What you said about going to discuss a job of work – I suppose that was all a lie. Well. I'm a fool and I believed you. But now I don't. And all I can say is, whoever you *have* been to see, I pity them if they're in half the state you are. You must have made a lovely pair."

His face, his very eyes, seemed to boil with fury. But he could not force himself to rise.

"Shut the cage of your ugly mouth. You always nag. You're a damned nagger. On and on you go. No wonder I don't want to be near you."

Something broke in Lucide. Not her heart, but something.

She scarcely knew what she did. But she found herself flying at him, her hands outstretched. Leaning over him as he sat, like a frenzied dancer in the jittery light, she clawed at his shirt, and beat with her hard small fists on his chest–"You filthy rotten drunken beast of a man –

how dare you tell me I'm to blame – how dare you have the gall to say that I–"

Her tirade ended as he rose abruptly against her and, pushing her back with his beefy curdled strength, next slapped the side of her face with the flat of his big hand.

Lucide reeled away. She half fell against the cabinet, and bottles rang and sprang. One tipped from the apron and smashed in a heap of wet fires – absinthe, lamplight, sugary glass.

Rage left her, even pain and despair. She was afraid. And yes, she had known terror also in her childhood.

Gui-Billy swayed, bracing himself against the sofa.

"I'm sorry I did that," he told himself, twice, in a slurred mumble. He seemed to be trying to convince himself of his regret. "But you asked for it, Luce–" Then he staggered and leant at a curious angle against the wall, shaking his dark tawny head. "Not going to argue any more. Why'd you make me keep arguing with you? I feel ill. You've made me ill."

His weakness lessened her fear. But also it reached deep into her, and twanged the ancient strings instrumentally built by God, presumably, into so many women. The animal imperative to care, and to protect – yes, even the beast that turns upon her. For it must be the master, and so in turn it will protect her from other, greater, shadows.

She approached him cautiously. Softly: "You'd better come and lie down. Do you want some water?"

"*No,*" he was vehement. "But I'll lie down."

"Not on that sofa. You won't be comfortable. Go upstairs. I'll help you, Gui–"

"Billy–" he grunted, uselessly.

She thought, *Oh God, perhaps I've been unfair. Perhaps he*

did see this man about work, and the man insulted him and let him down and Gui was so ashamed he went off drinking – yes, yes, it's that. What have I done but been harsh, when I swore I never would.

It was difficult to help support his burly weight all up the flight to the bedroom above. But patently he could hardly help himself.

When they reached the room, she led him, bowed and made to stagger too by his erratic movements, to the bed.

The lamp up here was burning low. It barely revealed her bruised left cheek, or the heap of turquoise silk and creamy lace that stretched across the pillows.

Gui-Billy crashed on to the bed.

Penitent, Lucide murmured, "You'll be uncomfortable like that. Let me help you take off some of your clothes–"

"Let me alone, can't you? Just leave me alone."

"Yes, then, very well... but – oh your shoes, Gui, the soles are so dirty – and they'll make your feet ache, just let me get them off–"

"Leave me alone, you brainless bitch – what are you, some trollop? I'm ill, damn you to Hell–"

Billy lurched upright and as Lucide backed hastily away, he began, without other preliminary, copiously to vomit. The stench of bile and second-hand alcohol infused the room. Already his garments, the covers of the bed, had received their tribute. But next, as if belatedly to recognise them, he grabbed up the nearest pillow, and with it, like a blue-green foamy phantom of some Heavenly sea, Lucide's nightgown and peignoir, continuing then to spew now solely on and into those, with an almost workmanlike and mechanical motion.

Over the night above and beyond the houses, the

churches, even higher than the upraised sphinx of the Cathedral, something is drifting, a filmy cloud, bluish perhaps – or more silvery? Surreal and amorphous, like a woman's most delicate shawl.

As it crosses the face of the moon, an instant of rose red colour seems to glint inside it. A ruby thought, one beat of a blood-red heart, or only the sheen of lamplight through wine. Gone now, anyway. Flown like the spirits of the birds in the Avenue of Opened Cages.

Act Two

Scene I

The chest in the armoire contained a great deal of money, in various coins and banknotes. He had tried to count it accurately and swiftly while no one was about. But, despite his skills in numeracy being far better than his literary ones, Billy was still uncertain he had the correct amount – and he was, in any case, only about half way through the hoard, while the clock now indicated four in the afternoon.

They would be here soon. He had better leave off and tidy up.

He replaced almost everything he had drawn out, and piled it back at least reasonably enough as he had found it. He kept to himself only one modestly lucrative paper worth two or three bottles, and perhaps some small placatory gift for Jeanne.

Then he shut the chest and pushed it well into the depths of the closet, after which he closed the doors.

Going to the window he looked out on to the street. No sign of them yet. It seemed they would be late deliberately, to rattle him. But it took more than that.

Billy thought of Jeanne suddenly, of how he had met her again that night more than a year ago. Of how he had gone to find her next, in the grocer's shop on the square. She had been measuring up little bags of coffee with, on her nose, the nippers of her spectacles – which seeing him, she snatched off at once.

This had amused him. Intent on a pursuit of her, he had not let his amusement show.

The other girl who worked there was out on an errand, but *she*, (this being Lucide Veilleur, the shop's proprietress), was apparently on the premises, as several times a week she always was. "Nosing around, trying to catch us out," as Jeanne summed it up.

He did not stay long therefore, but as he was leaving, Lucide came down from the upper storeroom, and he saw her.

Gui-Billy had, naturally, thought nothing of Lucide. She was in her forties he (wrongly) guessed, plain and rather un-pleasingly plump, and tradeswoman-proper, with an apron tied over her unfashionable dress. But later on, after Jeanne had been given the sack for theft, he recalled how Lucide had sent one or two attemptedly surreptitious glances at him. He prided himself on being able to read women like books, aside, evidently, from those times when they became so unreasonable as to be insane – during their courses, say, or pregnancy, or as they stopped being women at all and grew old. Beyond a certain age there was *no* knowing them, of course. But you could slough them before that, or you could if you had any sense.

Jeanne had become his mistress, but they had no money, none. Even clever thieves fell on hard times.

Therefore, at first without enlightening Jeanne, Billy went back to the shop on the square, and bought two or three cheap things, or pretended he would have bought them, if only he could find another job – an ungrateful dock overseer had got him thrown from his prior employment. (This lie had served Billy before.)

Lucide became infatuated, in love with him. Obviously she would, poor thing. Nearly thirty-eight, and a virgin. Had anyone ever even *looked* at her in the way he made out *he* did? He told her she was pretty, but not in the "coarse" way. He hoped she wouldn't mind him saying that... The sunlight on her hair made it shine, gave it real colour. And such big eyes (he privately thought them like the goggle eyes of a fish).

He intended to marry her, and get possession of her wealth. The plan was very simple. Having fleeced her, he would leave her. Yet it was a true work of art, what he did with her, the 'wooing'. He should give lessons. (Even Jeanne, after she got over her initial fury, had laughed at how he handled Lucide.)

But then, finally, it came to *this*. In the trap, and nothing to show for it. Or – not yet.

Outside, hoofs and carriage wheels. Presently downstairs the door bell jangled. He heard that little bitch Bette going to let them in.

Stuffing the note of money into a pocket, and all thought of the past out of his mind, he went to meet his in-laws.

They were in the downstairs parlour, Joséphe standing up and Grete already, uninvited, sitting in an armchair.

Joséphe Veilleur, at fifty, had a large, oblong, sallow face, deeply lined, a hooked nose, and a thin mouth that might, Billy had thought, indicate his miserly tendency, or only perhaps failing teeth. Joséphe's hair was gray, and his large watery eyes were some modest unnoticeable colour, like his sister's. But he stood straight, and waited politely, and when Lucide's young husband entered, Joséphe advanced and held out his hand.

"Good afternoon, Monsieur Milait. I hope you're well."

"Not bad. More impatient, really."

Joséphe Veilleur made no comment, but from the chair Grete gave off a little sharp hiss. If Luce had resembled *Grete* in any way, Billy had often thought, he could never even have touched her hand or kissed her cheek. She had northern blood, Grete, thin as a stick and hard as iron. A hard spiteful face too, but she dyed her hair dark brown, perhaps the colour it had been in her youth. It made her brows and lashes too light, bald-looking. A charming vision.

Joséphe acted as if neither Gui-Billy, nor Grete, had behaved in any unbecoming way.

"I expect Lucide told you we'd be calling here first, before going to see Lucide herself at the shop."

"No need for her to tell me. I read your letter to her." (This of course was not quite accurate. Rather Billy, after much trouble, had *pieced* the meaning together.)

Grete did more now than hiss. In a spiky metallic voice she said: "My husband's letter was addressed to Lucide, Monsieur Milait. It was private."

"Well, Madame, Luce is married to me. Nothing private between man and wife. I'm sure you agree, unless you're in the habit of keeping secrets from your husband here."

Grete rose. She stuck her head forward like a fighting cock. "I'm not having any more rudeness from you, you jumped-up nobody! If Lucide had ever listened to me, she'd never have married you. If *anyone* had listened, the marriage wouldn't have been allowed."

Joséphe spoke firmly. "Gretel, stop it, please." He always called her that, her full given name. "We're not here to quarrel." And Gretel-Grete put her head back into its normal position and sat down again. Joséphe nodded to Billy. "Might I sit, Monsieur?"

"Why not?"

As Joséphe took his place in another chair, Billy eyed the small notary's case Joséphe had brought with him. Joséphe did not put it down, but balanced it on one knee, like a pet he preferred to hold close to him. Billy went to a sideboard and removed a bottle of brandy, poured himself a measure, then hesitated. "Would you care for anything?"

Grete: "We're not in the habit of drinking spirits. Nor have we been offered them here before. But you have quite an array, I can see."

"Both here and upstairs," Billy nonchalantly replied. He downed his drink and poured another. Since the nasty turn on his Wedding Night four days had elapsed. He had been quite abstemious since, but his body now was healed and ready for alcohol.

Grete added, "*We* find drink of that sort far too costly."

"Oh? A short-sighted policy I'd say – what's the use of hoarding your money at your age? When you pass on, it won't go with you."

"*My age!*" This time she did not rise, but her dull face crimsoned. "I don't know how old you think I am–"

"Around the sixty mark."

At this, red went to magenta and up she dived again. Billy was tickled to see she could not, for a moment, speak at all.

Joséphe stirred gravely. "Calmly, Gretel. He's only joking."

"Oh, no, I'm being quite honest," Billy innocently reassured him.

Grete found her voice. "I'm not staying here to suffer his common jibes. I'm surprised you let him, Joséphe. Tell him what you've come here to say, and let's take our leave."

"Gretel, my dear, I can't explain it all that quickly to him. Things are rather complicated, as you know."

Grete was at the door. "Very well. I'll call down to the kitchen and get that useless Bette girl to make me a mint tisane to drink. Lucide treats her far too softly."

"You'll drink with the maid in the kitchen?" marvelled Billy.

"No, Monsieur Milait. I shall take my tea in Lucide's private parlour. You forget, I'm no stranger to this house. I've been here before ever *you* thrust your foot across the threshold."

"Well, if you care for a drop of absinthe," said playful Billy, "you'll find plenty in the cabinet up there. Not too much though, mind."

With another hiss, Grete left the room and they heard her sharp commands to Bette pitched over the banister, and then the swish of skirts ascending to the next floor.

Joséphe cleared his throat. "You must excuse Madame. She gets tetchy after a journey. Can I ask you to shut the door, if the maid's liable to go by? And I'll change my mind about that brandy."

Billy banged shut the door, poured an abstemious glass and handed it to Joséphe, then himself sat down beside the bottle. "So what's the mystery you have to explain to me?"

Joséphe straightened himself further. Abruptly businesslike, he regarded Billy with a steady, almost calculating look. Billy disliked this. He crossed his legs and began to turn his glass around.

"Before I explain anything, I must tell you that the reason I gave Lucide for calling on you first was not quite the real one."

"What–" Billy tensed – "you haven't brought the money?"

"Yes, I have the money here, in this case. This is the amount you requested, for your business venture, as you outlined it to Lucide. And in cash, as you also requested, which seems a little curious–"

"My partner required–" blurted Billy.

"Yes, your business partner – Monsieur... Jannier, I believe you said? Well, that is your affair, I suppose. But I've told Lucide only that I'd come here to discuss the venture, after which, all being well, I shall take her the money. My sister was very anxious that she, and so you, have funds as swiftly as possible. She's very pleased at the prospect that you should attain your own independence and prosperity." (Billy again averted nervous eyes from the wet, pebbly stare to which Joséphe was subjecting him.) "And, of course, this money *is* Lucide's, as you seem to have pointed out, and since she asked for it, I've complied. Those being the terms of our father's will."

Billy weakly said, "This is a good chance for me, you see, to set myself up – we could end with a fortune,

Jannier and me. Lucide won't mind that, will she?"

"I don't expect she will, Monsieur Milait. If it makes you happy. But..." Joséphe paused. He took another sip from his glass, "I want you to understand that it is highly important that this venture of yours works out. It will have to, Monsieur. No please don't interrupt me. There are no alternatives. You must make a *success*. If you don't, there is nothing more available to you. There'll be no more cash."

Billy pulled himself together. He had to stand up to this, not cower. "I reckon you've got the Devil's cheek to sit there and say my wife can't have any of her own money. Who do you think I am? Some boy, some child?"

"Did I say Lucide could have no more money? No, Monsieur, I said that *you* would get no more of it."

"She can do what she likes with her own money – and if I ask her, she'll give it to me."

"Which is why, in that event, she won't be given it. For her own use, yes. No more for you. Our father put me in a position to protect her, from *herself*, if you like. I can assure you, it's quite legal, even after her marriage. I'm able, if you want, to show you copies, notarised, signed, witnessed, of his wishes on this matter."

"Why do *you* need to protect her? She's married to me. *I* can do it."

Joséphe again cleared his throat. He drained the brandy, and set the glass down with great care.

"I'm afraid you can't. And now we arrive at the reason for my call on you today, which entails my explanation of why not."

"I believe my sister has told you that she was quite ill in childhood. Yes? Very well. Did she give you any details?

Did you yourself make any guesses? Typhoid? No, great Heaven, nothing like that. This sickness affected her mind, her spirit, even. I must draw in for you, Monsieur, the background.

"Lucide was a gentle, nervous girl, naive perhaps, happier with adults than with other children. Even I, of course, was twelve years her elder. She looked up to me, as to our father, though she was also a little afraid of him. To be truthful, as a boy, I was myself. He was, I confess, a strict man, but clever, and having our interests at heart. Our mother was long dead, alas. No doubt Lucide would have benefited from a mother's nurture...

"There was then a school, run for the daughters of the merchant class. Its reputation was sound, and to this, at the age of six, Lucide was sent. At first she did quite well. But then she drew, inadvertently no doubt, the attention of a coterie of unpleasant girls, two or three years her senior. Lucide was shy, and easily put out of countenance. Easily scared, too. You will know, children particularly can be very cruel. What? You say you had no trouble when a boy? I can believe it, Monsieur Milait. But Lucide was very far from being yourself.

"There was one girl, the leader of the little gang, of which there were six others. Her name was Martice – Martice Martin. Their circle was known as Martice and her Six Disciples. You can be sure the teachers disapproved of the slightly blasphemous reference! But they were also rather wary of Martice. Her father was quite a big noise in the woollen trade. He had given financial aid to the school.

"For about two years, as we later came to realise, Martice and her friends made Lucide's life miserable, maybe – I might even say – a waking nightmare. They would corner her at all opportunities, punch and pinch her, and pull her hair, while endlessly making fun of her and calling her by rude and contemptuous names. She'd been brought up gently enough, and a very little of this upset her very much. Among other things, she was forced to bring them 'offerings' – such items as fruit, or sweets from her own possession, presents they could, all of them, have gained, or had already been given, without any difficulty. Once they demanded one of her dolls they had overheard her speaking of with affection. She duly rendered it to them and they broke it in pieces in front of her. All this while they threatened that if she told anyone the extent of their tortures, they would do much worse. It seems Martice vaunted herself, saying she had magical powers, and would unleash monsters and evil imps to punish my sister. Lucide was only eight, and credited every word.

"Well now. One day Martice and her company decided on another scheme. When the pupils were released for the day, they forced Lucide into the school garden. Here the cronies held her captive while Martice carried out the latest diversion. It seems they had dreamed it up some time before, but must now carry it out, because, as Martice told my sister, Lucide was so ugly she was unbearable. And so Martice would improve Lucide's looks in the way women of the streets did it. Lucide had dreaded this act some while. But now it was performed. With a stick of rouge and another of black kohl – God knows how they had got hold of such stuff – Martice daubed scarlet and then black streaks and blotches all over my sister's face and neck. When all was complete to their satisfaction, they showed Lucide to herself in a mirror. After which they let her go.

"Perhaps this doesn't sound so much to you, Monsieur. But I was at home that day, and saw the result, and it was, you must credit me, quite terrible, somehow really horrible – Lucide looked as if she had been exposed to some frightful plague or similar illness, even one that was – *sexual* in origin – or else as if she had been cut, scalded, burnt. The poor little girl ran home screaming, and reaching the house she continued to scream. No one could stop her, no one could learn what had caused the awful marks – except, thank God, that they were applied rather than *physical*. Lucide rushed about the house, tearing out handfuls of her own hair, and making these alarming cries. The physician was sent for. But before he arrived, quite suddenly, Lucide grew silent and dropped to the ground. She was unconscious. And she remained so. Even the doctor, when he came in and assured us Lucide was alive – we hadn't been sure – was yet unable to revive her.

"She lay on her bed, Monsieur, for seven days, like a broken doll. Lifeless, however, she was not. It was nearly impossible to see, but she breathed. And once the muck was washed off, her skin... it was *gray*. Never in my life, before or since? have I seen living skin that colour, not even in the very elderly or diseased. Gray – like fish-skin. Even now... as you can see it distresses me. Pour me another brandy, if you will, Monsieur. I must finish my story."

Seven days the child, lying in her coma, barely breathing, with a heartbeat faint as the whisper of a feather. Face and neck, hands and arms and feet, (and all the hidden rest), like dull pewter. No movement behind the lids. No movement at all. She must be turned manually at intervals, and washed. (Peculiarly, both her hired nurses recorded that Lucide gave no evidence of bodily functions. No material of any sort issued from her that needed cleansing.) They moistened her lips, but her lips stayed dry. She was cold to the touch. Neither stiffened nor limp. Like a bale of cloth... She could not survive.

Other physicians entered the house and talked to the elder Monsieur Veilleur, a practical and knowledgeable man. It would be better to consign this child to a hospital. Or, perhaps, to some big brick citadel of an asylum that roosted in the valley-pits of the City, one of three appalling madhouses, of which so many ghastly tales were related. For even should the child return to life, her brain, by now, would be irreparably damaged, her mind derailed. She must and would be a lunatic. Where else then than the madhouse should she go?

Practical old Monsieur Veilleur thought otherwise. For one thing he was well aware that the madhouse cost a lot of money, if one wished one's relatives at all looked after in it. (And frankly, even those whose stay was financed, fared poorly, or so he had been led to believe.) Monsieur Veilleur valued a proper return for a reasonable investment. His son too, Joséphe, was in his stolid way apparently unnerved at the idea of the asylum. Fathers and sons involved together in commercial enterprise had better not fall out.

All this might have caused talk in the City, at least among those classes and in those areas where such persons as the Veilleurs were noticed.

However, their misfortune, it turned out, had been thoroughly upstaged.

The very night of Lucide's distraught return and subsequent lapse into coma, a dire and incredible murder was discovered in the neighbourhood. The facts of this crime,(which it transpired would never be solved, the perpetrator never captured), were so extreme as generally not to be accepted. Besides, the six witnesses to the event were themselves in a pitiable state. What had killed the seventh of their number in such an unspeakable manner had wounded and afflicted also them. Worst of all, they were all female and all children, the oldest only eleven years of age.

"You ask why I mention this crime, Monsieur Milait. Well, it's a curiosity, and a disgusting one, but it saved my family some unwanted social scrutiny, Lucide especially, since all talk at that time concerned this murder. But the young girls harmed and killed, most oddly, were none other than Martice and her cronies. And ironically, you may think, it was those six accomplices of hers who ended up in the madhouse, all but one, who threw herself in the river. They'd all been maimed, you see, in the attack. Ripped across the face and so on, and their arms and legs broken in many places. All had been scarred for life. Some could never walk after. They had been in the school garden still, probably gloating over their treatment of my sister. A caretaker found them that evening, about nine o'clock, and a frightful scene it was. It nearly drove him mad as well. But the wretched children were crazed without a doubt. All six of them swore it was nothing human, but a *demon* that had killed Martice and next injured them.

"But we soon enough lost track of the case anyway, for on the eighth morning my sister woke from her trance. And, just as predicted, it seemed she was herself half mad. She knew us, and where she was, yet she couldn't remember a single moment of her last weeks at the school. Instead she began to protest that she must go there at once. She was cheerful, and very nearly determined, something unusual in Lucide. She said she did not want to be late, and that her friends would be anxious about her – whereas, unfortunately, she had, you see, no true friends at the school. While in our efforts to learn more about what had happened to precipitate her collapse, I had looked over her personal journal. And I'd seen there descriptions of the vicious behaviour of Martice, and how Lucide had been made too frightened to reveal it to others. Soon I spoke to Lucide, as perhaps I think now I should not have done, about the bullying, and the red and black scrawled on her face. At this she only shook her head in surprise. We had next, almost with force, to prevent her from going out. It took a sedative at last to make her docile. She recovered during the following days, but even when otherwise seemingly restored to herself, she still could not recall Martice, nor her accomplices. She had forgotten them so completely they might never have existed.

"This forgetfulness the doctors classed as a serious symptom of her illness. And through the years certainly Lucide has never recaptured any memory of her tormentors. She believes she was fairly happy at school, and was removed from it only due to poor health. Other things she recollects quite normally.

"We were strongly advised after all of this, and by all of the doctors who had attended her, that we should therefrom watch and protect Lucide. She received tuition in the house, and later, under my father's guidance, learned to be a decent businesswoman, able to manage the grocery shop in which he set her up. On his death she inherited this property on the Avenue, and made her home here. Lucide, I must assure you, has been exemplary all these years, in all things, though by nature she's stayed a quiet little women, preferring to keep to herself. And then, as we know, Monsieur Milait, she met you.

"What you'll have to grasp now, Monsieur, is that my father's guard of her passed to me, and I shall maintain it, while I live. This is for Lucide's own sake, and until now she has prospered by it. I have to tell you, too, despite there being no relapse in the thirty years since, we were warned she would remain, in her own way, fragile. It has been a rule for me that nothing serious should ever be allowed to upset her, nothing must *harm* her. It is stated in my father's will. I state it now. I hope you, now, will see the sense of it."

Billy, who had sat there with his mouth ajar, filled the gap with brandy, swallowed, and said flatly, "If I'd known any of this I'd never have married her."

The door flew open. Grete had returned, and some while previously it seemed. Like a spider she must noiselessly have crept down to listen. Loudly she said: "And it's no thanks to me you weren't told. I've entreated Joséphe to tell you, and been ignored."

Joséphe spared her not a glance. He said to Billy, "We've no cause to worry. Monsieur Milait knows the situation now. I'm sure it's been a bit of a shock to him, but he is Lucide's husband, and will, as I have and shall, do his utmost for her. He'll know," Joséphe added, pebble eyes slightly reddened but still intransigently fixing Billy, "that if this marriage turns out a happy one, it'll be the making of my sister."

"We'll have to say our prayers for that, then," said

Grete.

Billy snapped back into himself and glared at her.

"And if she and I were happy you'd hate that, wouldn't you, Madame?"

Grete turned to face the stair. She said as she went out, "I am leaving now, Joséphe. Please escort me."

"In a moment. You go down, I'll follow you in a minute, Gretel."

Again that tiny hiss, less a serpent perhaps than steam expelled from an overloaded faucet.

Joséphe got up, and tucked the notary's case under his left arm. "Well, I'll deliver this to Lucide now. So I'll say goodbye till next meeting. Treat my sister kindly, Monsieur. She's a good woman. She'll make you a loyal and loving wife. She deserves nothing of you but the best. She's never hurt another. She shouldn't herself be hurt."

Again then, he held out his hand.

Billy, frowning, squirming, raging, sweating, shook it.

And Joséphe went out and down the stairs, to join his atrocious dyed wife in their expensive carriage.

Scene 2

When Lucide entered the house, the clock on the market church was striking seven, and the sky beyond the house had become a syrupy yellow. The hot, dusty day was wandering ignorantly to its close.

Inside the hallway Lucide hesitated, and looked up the stairs. No lamp was yet lit, and no one seemed about. Reluctant to call to Bette, who was probably napping, Lucide left the packages she had brought on a table. She only kept hold of her usual bag of faded embroidered cloth.

The house was so thickly quiet. Had he gone out again? He had been out every night, for a walk, he had told her. To clear his head. He was never back in less than three hours. He had not been drinking, but that seemed now to make him more morose than when inebriated. And, too, he had not touched her. Not touched her, that was, as a lover. She had told herself he had been worried about getting the money for this business deal, which it appeared he had struck after all – on the night he came back drunk – and ruined her nightgown – that lovely silk – and she had had to throw it away since it was beyond cleaning – and torn too, where he had clutched it – not in passion, but nausea

On the landing above a looming shape appeared. It was Gui, and somehow the shadows had enlarged him.

He greeted her with a sullen "You're late."

"Only half an hour. Joséphe and I were talking."

"What about?" He sounded resentful and suspicious.

But of course, he had some cause to be anxious.

"Oh, just silly family things from years ago. He's my brother, we sometimes reminisce. I've got the money."

"I know, don't I? He was here first, wasn't he?"

"Yes... I hope you were civil to him, Gui."

"We got on splendidly. But I nearly threw that witch Grete out of a window."

"She annoys everyone."

"A crack on the jaw would improve her. He must be a weakling, to put up with it."

Lucide had stopped on the stair but now she continued to climb upward. He did not move, either towards her or to allow her to go by. So she stopped again, standing on the step just below the landing.

"Gui – did he ask you a lot of questions?"

"No, he seemed more ready to tell me things–" Billy hesitated. He should not, presumably, reveal to her what Joséphe had told. Billy amended quickly "–like exactly how I should handle the deal I've made. I played along. But I know Jannier, and Joséphe doesn't."

"I'll come up then, wash my hands and face, and then I'll go and organise Bette. We must have our dinner–"

"Confound dinner. What about my money."

Despite the rest, she gasped. She felt so tired. What a hot and heavy evening, She wanted to sit down for a little. Just sit down and be still. She had even put off Joséphe, offering to bring her back in the carriage. "What about the money? I said I have it."

"Well, so you've got it. Aren't you going to hand it over?"

"Gui–"

"*Billy* – for Christ's sake – *Billy*–"

"Billy. Give me a chance to catch my breath. Let me get by, let me have a moment. And I'll give it to you."

He moved back and she stepped up on to the landing. Instantly he said, "Hand it over, then."

"G – Billy – please. I've done everything you asked. Please don't spoil things now. Not now."

"Spoil what? I'm not spoiling anything. Why are you holding back?"

Lucide walked past him and up the further flight to her own parlour above.

He bawled after her, "You haven't answered me yet!"

But she had gone into the upper room. She said nothing.

Billy bounded up the stairs, noisy and purposeful. He sprang into her parlour, and there she sat, her pinned-up hair dishevelled, her worn workaday bag on her lap. What a lump she looked. How had he stood even this much of her?

"What's this?" he said loudly, "you don't reply to my questions now? You'd better see some sense."

"Oh Gui," she said sadly, drearily. "Gui, please don't shout at me–"

"Then speak up. If you're trying to play some game, it isn't to my taste, you hear? Don't think you can mess me around."

"I wanted so much," she said, in the same wretched tone, "for us to have a nice time this evening. Despite everything. I'd wanted to look forward to us sharing an evening – but then – well. Listen, dear Gui – I'm sorry, dearest Billy – I need to have a little talk with you before I give you the money. That's not unreasonable. Not under the circumstances. So don't start to make me miserable the moment I come in. Let me take a little rest. I've had a bit of – I've had a tiring day."

On a table stood a cup with, Billy assumed, the dregs of the mint tisane Grete had wanted. A slip of paper lay under the saucer. Billy, mistrusting any note that harpy might have left, moved towards it, shifted the china and peered, trying to translate the words.

"What's this?"

"Oh, it's from Grete. She says Bette told her she must go home, her mother was ailing–"

"That worthless slut's idiot of a mother is always ailing – according to Bette. A pack of lies. You should throw her out, get a proper worker, and a decent cook, too. Bette can't cook, and nor can you, I've learnt that to my cost."

"Perhaps. I'm sure you're right. Now please–"

Billy, as if dismissing them all, crossed the room to the

cabinet. No drink stood out on its apron, but flinging back the door he withdrew a fresh bottle of brandy.

Lucide watched him as he freed the cork and drank directly from bottle's mouth, with the hunger of a baby taking suck.

"Please don't drink, Gui – Billy. Not tonight. I particularly didn't want you to."

"Why not? What else am I to do? No food, no money – I might as well have some brandy."

"It made you so ill when you kept having it... last time."

"A couple of drinks isn't to 'keep having it'. And this is brandy not that cheap absinthe you got in."

"It's more than a couple of drinks. Grete said you were drinking this afternoon."

"That bloody God-blasted hag needs shooting. I'd like to get a revolver and see to it myself. Do the district – all bloody Marcheval a favour."

"Please don't start. Let's be peaceful, just for a while. I've done my very best to help you, to make you happy. But – Well. I'll go straight down and cook us some supper. That's best. Just something simple. Yes. I'll do that."

She rose, as if absentmindedly carrying the bag with her, went out and down the stairs, all the way down to the kitchen region.

Billy stood glaring into space. His eyes in the gathering of the dark burned almost red. The hand that did not hold the bottle was clenched to deliver a blow. Bloody interfering, dithering cows, all of them – but *this* one – well, a lunatic. Joséphe had said. "*Mind derailed.*" And he, the brainless numbskull, had blundered into a marriage with her. And he had thought his plan foolproof! All he could see now was the chest upstairs in the armoire. Why not go up, while Luce got on with concocting some slop in the kitchen, go up and empty the chest and make a run for it? Jeanne was right. Damn the rest of the money, and damn Luce –

Just then the doorbell made its jangling, dropped-cutlery signal to the unlit house.

Going to a window Billy heaved it upward and leaned out. There on the step below was a dirty urchin from the lower streets, looking right up at him and grinning crooked teeth.

Billy made a grunting sound.

He knew the boy.

The wretch lived near *The Piping Clown* and now and then performed errands for Jeanne.

Billy indicated that the boy must move away and off down the avenue, then he, Billy, would come out to meet him.

With luck, *she* would not have heard the bell. He had noticed her hearing was not as acute as a younger woman's, and banging about in the kitchen would have aided the omission. (Bette frequently failed to hear the doorbell, and so answer the door, when cooking.)

Luck held. Lucide either had not heard or had left reaction to Billy.

He opened the front door and went out.

The sky now was burning up with a parchment-coloured fever-fire. Buildings stuck black on the raw sear of it, and the slum-child had hidden so well behind the silhouette of a tree, Billy thought for a second he was gone.

"This is a creepy street, Monsieur Billy," the boy said, when found. "All those cages standing open and all over rust. I want to get off I do, before those ghost-birds start their flying around, like they say they do."

"Then tell me why you're here, and make it quick."

"Give me a coin."

Billy snarled but he knew the rules of the slum and the wharf. He took out a coin and held it up in the air, where the final death-throes of the day changed it to a molten bullet.

"You first."

"There's some man that's the friend of her husband, Antoine-in-the-Prison, and he wants to come and see her about some scheme he's got for when Antoine gets home. And she doesn't want to be in the house when this friend turns up. So she says you've got to come to her early and take her off somewhere for the evening, till Antoine's friend gives up."

"Tell her I can't. Not tonight."

The boy grinned again. Like the coin, his snaggle teeth, catching the dying light, flared, filthy flames, tiny molten knives –

"She says to me if you say that I must say: Tell Billy to come here, or I'll go *there*. I'll come and see him and his wife. That's what Jeanne said. Now, I've done my bit, so give me my coin."

"Here. Go back and say I can't. There's good reasons. Say it's to do with the *gift* I was expecting today. I can't leave until I've got it."

Snatching the coin, the child spun about and bolted away along the avenue, the last faded-black reflections of trees and pillars and cages striping and mottling him until, with a sudden peculiar *blink*, all light went out in night.

Her useless maid-cook, Bette, had seemingly left some soup. This, heated up, Lucide brought into the small dining room, with bread and cheese and a solitary bottle of red wine. She must already have gone into the room, since candles were burning on the table, and the gas-lamps, (not prevalent through the upper parts of the. house) had also been lit.

She had drawn the velvet curtains too. The street was invisible, the City, the world.

Just the two of them, then.

"What concoction's that?" he inquired, drinking his brandy.

"It's a nice soup with onions and meat. We've eaten it before. You had no complaints."

Did she offer a touch of asperity? *She – Luce –*

Squash it, quick!

"Some muck. All I expect here. I don't want it. Besides, I have to go out."

Having put down her tray, Lucide left the table and went across the room to stand not three feet from him.

"Not now, Gui. You're not going out tonight."

"And you're going to stop me, I suppose."

Somehow, in a move he had not noted, she had regained her shabby embroidered bag. She held it to her and tapped it. "*This* will stop you. The money's in here. If you want that you won't go out. This is my night, Gui. I've never had my night. I'm going to claim it, Gui. No, forgive me, I'm going to *have* it, *Billy*."

Billy's jaw dropped. He drew it up.

She looked as ever. Plump, sagging, unimportant, old and female. And yet. What in God's name had got into her? His spine had gone cold, only an instant, but *palpably*. *She* wanted and would have. *She*. And, for that splinter of time, had he believed she might?

He was caught between one madwoman and another. Bloody lunatic Luce – and crazy feral Jeanne, demanding and desperate, liable – oh, he thought so – to come rushing up here with her cries and threats.

"I do have to go out, Luce." He sounded placatory. Well, that was a precaution. "Jannier – he's up in arms, thinks I've been bluffing – partly your fault, too, since you haven't given me anything in the financial way to show him. So I need to go and – *explain*. I won't be long. I'll be back as soon as I can."

"As you were soon back," she said, tonelessly, "on our Wedding Night."

"Listen, woman. It's no good arguing. I have to go out and–"

"You must listen to *me*, Billy. You think I'm a fool, and you're right. I have been, where you're concerned. I couldn't help myself, but I've had my lesson."

Something in her eyes made him stare. It was almost like the unsettling afterglow outside, the coin like the bullet, the teeth that reminded him of molten metal. He had never seen real colour in her eyes before, nor did he now. But they too were metallic, he thought. A sort of tin, gray... silver-gray...

"If you go out tonight," she said, "to see this person, or for one of your *walks*, I tell you now: it won't matter how long or how quick you are with them, because I won't let you back in. Leave me tonight, and I'll lock and bar every door and window. You will never enter this house again. I mean it, *Billy-Gui*. I am as serious as death itself,"

On the table, the soup cooled in a dull pall of defeated red meat.

"Come and sit down, Billy, for a moment. It won't make anything easier, you pacing up and down."

Billy stopped. His face was flushed and wooden.

"If you knew about me and her, why didn't you come out with it before? Why did you leave it to – *fester*?"

"I didn't know about it. As I told you, I was simply uncomfortable, a sort of premonition. She'd made it obvious herself, if I think of it now. Suddenly always taking those nipper-spectacles of hers off, and rubbing the top of her nose to get rid of the pink mark, and always when a man a bit like you started across the square. Well. Perhaps not so often, but often enough. And once or twice it *was* you, and then her face took on a certain look. Oh, you think I don't know anything, but I do know how a woman looks when she likes a man. I've seen it, *felt* it on my own face, haven't I, if nothing else. And then, when I'd sent her packing for stealing all those bits and pieces – and *you* started to come in anyway and make up to me – oh, don't be mistaken, I *loved* that. My heart used to – it used to open like a flower. A poor silly flower that thought spring had happened, didn't realise winter was just around the corner–"

"But you didn't know," impatiently, angrily he interrupted this theatrical flight of fancy, "you never knew that she and I had known each other before."

"No, I didn't know that. Well, now I know that too, don't I. Oh Billy, when you started all those *walks* at night, three hours away or more. I knew *then*, if not *who*. I knew on the night of the day I married you, you went off to some other woman. How could you, Gui, how *could* you? What a wicked, *vicious*, *heartless* thing to do to someone that loved you so."

"*She* loves me," he rapped out. "I suppose she doesn't

matter."

"I know *I* don't," Lucide answered. "I never did."

He said: "Plenty of men take a mistress, and the wife puts up with it, doesn't fuss. A little sweet on the side of the plate, as they say. A man likes a change."

"A change? A change from what? You've never even kissed me, Gui. Not once, in the loving way."

"So then, *I've not kissed you*!" he shouted. "Why bring all this out now?"

Lucide folded her arms more closely over her bag. She held it like a crushed baby to her breast.

"I was late home, wasn't I? You snapped at me about it. In fact it wasn't because I was chatting to my brother. After he'd gone and I was about to lock up the shop, a last customer came in. I won't tell you who, but she told me she'd seen you and Jeanne Croll together in that public house near the river. Yesterday. During that time when you were 'walking'. My customer is a rough woman, but she always pays and is polite. She said too Jeanne Croll is a whore by trade and nature, and a slut, and her husband is a pig, and soon due to leave the prison. He is the violent type. She warned me you were in danger if you were carrying on with Jeanne, and I should look out for you, and for myself, because no doubt Madame Croll was riddled with diseases you might pass on to me. *Slight chance*! I nearly laughed."

Inconsequently yet belligerently, Billy retorted, "Jeanne's clean as the inside of an apple."

"Let's hope so then, for *your* sake. But that's how I know. And that's what I wanted to talk to you about, your affair, before I give you all this money. I need to know what you're going to do now."

He squared his big shoulders.

"What I'm going to do is go out and speak to Jannier–"

"Oh! *Jannier*! Couldn't you have coined a better name than that, *Gui-Billy*. *Jeanne – Jannier* – I saw through that the moment my customer told me who she was. *Is* there even a business venture? I doubt it. Joséphe doubted it, too, not to mention that viper Gretel."

"Right, you're very clever, Luce. Now listen carefully. Jeanne needs me tonight – if you know about us you'd better hear this. I have to go to her, because she sent me a threatening message–"

"Yes, I heard the doorbell. I looked up from the basement window. That poor little boy with bare feet. He was from her, was he? I partly guessed."

"But you don't understand, do you, so shut your mouth and take this in. If I don't go to *her* she'll come *here*. She's half off her head worrying about that convict husband of hers. And she's half your age and ten times stronger, I shouldn't wonder. Do you want a wild cat scratching your door down?"

Lucide had turned even paler than she already had been. It made her eyes far richer in colour. Like silver they looked now, iridescent, and the pupils jet-black stars.

"Let her, then. Perhaps it's the best way. You and me and her. We'll have it out, once and for all. I tell you, Billy, she's not having you. She already has a husband, someone even more selfish and cruel than you, it seems. But you're mine, Gui. *Mine*, Billy. I'm your *wife*. And I'm going to keep you, even if I have to *buy* you with every last franc I have in the world."

Billy gaped at her. And then he swung about to the door. He kept the brandy bottle tight in his hand too, just as Lucide had kept hold of her bag of money.

"Good for you then, Lucide. But I'm off. I'll take my

leave. You two squalling mad cats can fight it out alone. Sort it out yourselves. Maybe I'll see you later. Oh, and bolt and bar the place if you want. If I *mean* to get in, I can always manage it."

"You coward," she whispered.

"No. I'm the only sane one here." And he went hurriedly through the doorway. She heard, as so often, the clatter of his footfalls, and then the front door opened, next slammed like thunder, so the old house vibrated as if struck a violent blow.

Act Three

Scene I

Lucide is in her own upper parlour, before the pier glass. She has lit the painted lamp, and indeed has lit all the lamps in her house. Now it glows to the avenue outside, like a beacon. One of the windows in this room stands open, and the curtain a little wide, so she can hear any noise in the street. But so far all she can make out are the dim whirring sounds and the miniature twittering fountains of birdsong that, occasionally, many of the inhabitants of the Avenue of Aviaries detect. (Once, years back, she had thought she heard one of the ghostly parrots reciting, on the ledge by her bedroom, fragments of what might have been a classical poem. She had slept alone in those days. As, in reality, she still does.)

She has not changed her clothes, still wears her ordinary dress. But she has washed her face – the bruise he made has faded, a good thing, or Grete would have been sure to remark on it. And now, rather than pin up her hair again, Lucide has let it down, and is brushing it, slowly. As is quite common when a woman brushes her hair, blue sparks fly up from it with an intermittent crackle.

And set loose, Lucide's hair is a revelation. (Few have seen it like this since her childhood.) Long, nearly to her waist, in natural colour a sort of ashy light brown, it is dense yet silken, and gleams from the attentions of the brush, giving off a faint aroma like sage, new grass and fragrant powders .

But now there is another sound. Not living hair, nor the phantom birds.

(In a strange, almost profligate act, Lucide has previously gone down and undone her front door, then left it ajar. The strategy perhaps of someone who has passed beyond all care, a deed of desperation – or defiance... or utter fearlessness?)

And the sound Lucide has heard at last is that of a light step entering her house through that open door. And then a woman's voice, young and sharp, calls upward: "Billy? Are you there?"

Lucide puts down the brush and goes out to the stair.

She calls in turn down through the house.

"Come in, Madame Croll. Do come up. I've been waiting for you."

"Where's Billy?" Jeanne demanded as she walked into the upper parlour.

"My husband has gone out. He didn't want to see you. But we don't need him here. We can say whatever we've got to say without him listening."

"There's nothing to talk about. I've come here for Billy.

If he's not here then there's no reason I'd stay. Where's he gone? Oh, but then, I doubt *you'd* know. He doesn't think enough of you, does he, to tell you where he goes."

"And what do you think he thinks of you, Jeanne? He reckons you're some dirty little whore that he can play about with in his spare time. *Something on the side of his plate*, as he put it. However, he's married now, and you'll just have to make do with your own delightful husband."

Jeanne stood half at bay, half primed to attack, in the doorway of Lucide's parlour. Her bright green eyes had already taken in, with dubious, scornful avidity, the house's many bourgeois comforts and riches – so many lamps and candles, clocks, carpets, wallpapers, velvet drapes. Some burglar could make a proper killing in here. But that was nothing to do with Jeanne. Jeanne's mission was clear, to find her feckless but irresistible lover. She ignored Lucide's jibe. Ignored the slight difference to Lucide, the let-down electricity of her hair – Jeanne stayed with the pith of Lucide's words.

"*Married*? What – to *you*? No one'd call that a marriage. Some legal garble mouthed in a civil ceremony to a bored clerk – and then you think Billy's going to be tied to a woman looks old enough to be his mother. All he ever wanted from you was your money, tiny mean little hoard as it is – and he, the damned fool, never saw he wouldn't get it. Married to you!" Jeanne, melodramatically spiteful, threw back her head to jeer. "You'd have to be a madwoman if you think a man like him would ever stay with you, even if you fed him five million francs every day. He's *young*. He *wants* someone young."

(Something in Lucide, after all, was changing, or reverting. Her lips drooped. Did she tremble? A child's face, uncertain and afraid, daunted, done for.)

But she said: "Gui – Billy – is mine. You always were a thief, but you won't steal *him*. He married *me*. He doesn't want *you* any more – so you can get out of this house, and out of his life, and stay out. If he cared so much for you, do you think he'd have gone out and left me here to meet you? No. He asked me to tell you, Jeanne, that what you had is all finished. Is over. So. You'd better leave at once."

Despite these positive words, this grieving child does not convince.

Hard-headed Jeanne can see as much.

"You've got it wrong, Madame, not me. Billy didn't stay because he's a coward. I wouldn't even be surprised if he *is* here. *Hiding*. I thought I might need my spectacles, my nippers, so I brought them. Oh, you'll recall those, won't you. But at least I've got a pair of eyes too, not like you. I'm sure you thought it very funny that I was shy of putting them on. But you'd do better with a pair, to cover your eyes *up*, you bloody fish-eyed thing!"

Without more preface, Jeanne the wild cat, the feral lynx, springs forward, and seizing Lucide by the shoulders, shakes her with brutal efficiency.

A strange lost cry breaks from Lucide.

It is like the repetition of another cry, but one voiced long ago. Thirty years before, maybe. Horror and affront; outrage, despair –

Jeanne, (as she shakes and *shakes* Lucide – like annoying washing?): "Now, you bitch, where *is* he? I'm not leaving this sewer of a house until I see him – till I *rescue* him – where's my Billy hiding?"

Lucide is limp in her grasp.

Jeanne slaps Lucide's face, not as violently, certainly, as Billy had done, but violently enough. Sufficient, as they say .

Jeanne: "*Now*, where is he? Come on, you eyesore, *tell* me. All right, you bloody sow, I *will* search the place from end to end. I'll put on my nippers and look in every drawer for keys – you've tricked him and locked him in somewhere, I'll bet, you Godforsaken old crone – who gave you the right to say what can happen for him, or for me?"

And Jeanne then, moved beyond even her most virulent impulse, rakes Lucide's cheek with her hard, sharp lynx's claws.

Blood springs out. And with a kind of disgust, partly at Lucide, and also, unrecognised, somewhat at herself – Jeanne dances away.

She looks around her (wildly) and then rushes out, pouncing up the stairs to the top floor below the attic, where the bedroom waits.

Lucide stands still in her parlour.

One side of her face, the left side where, days ago, Billy had struck her, is vivid again with thin running trickles of blood. It is not too bad, it will not scar. That is, it will not scar physically.

She does not seem to know what to do, Lucide. Then, rather drearily, she moves back to the mirror. Again she looks at herself, and the encarnadined cheek, the rouge-red, and the kohl-black shadow that her long hair shades it with.

Suddenly her face breaks into a gargoyle grimace of weeping, but there are no tears, and the grimace lasts less than seven beats of her heart. After which her face slackly relaxes.

Her slack mouth opens then and lets out a noiseless scream. As if air had been released to create a vacuum .

And after that something seems to release her. to

disconnect all the marionette strings which, until this second, have been holding her upright. As if she were only a pile of discarded clothing, (the shaken washing?) and a blot of hair unrelated, (a wig, perhaps) Lucide slides to the floor.

And lies there motionless, and seemingly unbreathing. *Like a broken doll.*

A broken doll.

Upstairs in Lucide's bedroom, Jeanne is poised. A lamp blazes in here, as everywhere else, and Jeanne's expression is one of rabid frustration as she glares at all the furnishings and luxuries she herself has never known – and which are, all of them, quite empty of Billy.

Then she takes note of the tall broad armoire. One door is slightly ajar, rather as the front door to the house had been. He is in the clothes closet then, the cowardly bastard.

Jeanne creeps to the armoire, and wrenches wide both doors. Ranks of clothes slap out at her, stupid, unglamorous clothes, she thinks, chosen by an old and unloved frump. In a contempt amounting almost to allergy, Jeanne begins to push them aside.

Suddenly she shrieks.

Jeanne shrieks in pain, shock and terror, and even as she does so she beholds a shower of scarlet blood that shoots right by her, in at the closet doors, spattering several of the hanging garments. But Jeanne is crazily clutching at them for support. Does she realise the blood is her own, carved out of her back and side? Perhaps not, yet.

But she does seem afraid to turn, she seems afraid to, though moaning now, whimpering, she does turn. She faces round to the room, and sees what has been behind her. And is now in front.

"What–? *What*–? God– Christ– No– Oh God– *no– no–*"

Something is there.

But what?

What is there?

What is it that has torn that massive wound in Jeanne's back, passing so easily through cloth and corset, through skin and flesh? What is it that is once more reaching out for Jeanne, like an infant, perhaps, reaching after a beloved toy–?

The lamp burns magnificently, and shows everything in the room so very well, almost like a painting in oils. But, as in a painting too, maybe, the colours all a little heightened, or changed in their tint – the dark wood like carmine flowers, the pastel covers like blue ice, brown to amber and to bottle-glass green, gray to purple... even the shadows have colours in them, crimson, orange, violet –

And in the middle of it all, a silver thing. Pure silver as if only just made, burnished, some wonderful ornament from some huge necklace or brooch. It slowly twists and turns, like a giant fish in glowing water, catching all the shades and highlights and tints on its scales. For it *is* scaled, as a fish would be, or a snake. Possibly it has more of the snake to it, and yet, from the serpentine body, silver forearms have risen, delicate silver *hands*, each with seven fingers – and the long-necked head – that is nearly human – but more beautiful, much more. A perfect face, with dark silver eyes and a rose-red mouth, red as if exquisitely coloured in by the finest lip-rouge. And its hair swirls, tendrils of flexible silver and platinum. It gleams and shines, swims and twists and sways. But also it is winged. Vast wings, wider than those of an eagle, they brush the walls to either side, and they have feathers, the most delicate though enormous, each one sculpted from the silver metal. As they flutter, they produce the mildest flittering of rhythmic noise, like a musical accompaniment to some unheard song.

Transfixed by fiery agony and bewildered terror, Jeanne is sinking backward. But the fabulous creature now catches her, arresting her fall. After which it holds Jeanne firmly, paying no heed to her feeble struggles, and all the while – with a sort of tender and involved interest– it begins to break all the bones that are in Jeanne's arms and fingers, in her ribcage, her pelvis and her legs.

The screams resume, of course they do.

The screams go on, but fortunately the windows up here have not been undone, the curtains are closed, and no one else is in the house, thus nobody at all will be disturbed by them.

When everything is broken, every bone, the silvery creature shreds Jeanne's face, until it is a curious mask of scarlet and black, where the green eyes, like two green suns, are now setting forever.

With a final flick of one hand, the creature snaps Jeanne's neck.

The work is complete. Silence has returned. Into the armoire the wreckage of Jeanne is lightly slung, far back, where the money chest is. And the bloodied clothes swing over, but cannot entirely cover Jeanne. But then the doors are shut. And the lamp flickers, steadies. And the colours in the room alter to their normal everyday hues.

Outside, the clock of the market church strikes for ten.

Where ever does time fly to?

The bedroom is vacant, as is the rest of the house, apart from Lucide.

Lucide, lying unconscious below on the floor of her parlour. And for a moment there too, a flicker, like the lamp-flicker above, and from her mouth, a whisper? If anyone had been beside her, they would not have heard it. They never had. What has she said?

Now Martice, that will stop you. No one to help you now, Martice Martin.

Scene 2

Just past midnight, Gui Billy Milait reached the door of Lucide's house.

There was nothing in any way surprising, since Jeanne had shut the door on entering. Otherwise, there were lamps burning, though not the gas-lamps on the ground floor. Only a collective of thundery heat, and the resultant pervasive reek of the evening's meat soup, spoiled the hallway. Everything otherwise seemed mundane and orderly. He hoped to God it was.

Billy thought he should not have run away – because God knew what he would have to put up with now. But Lucide had not stuck to her vow to lock him out... And perhaps bloody Jeanne had also come to her senses. If nothing had happened, Lucide had probably gone to bed. He thought she had meant to go to the shop again tomorrow, and would need an early night. Even if he saw her in the morning, he could fob her off, wait till she left, and then take the money, what she had brought him – if she really had – and everything in the chest. After that he would make his escape.

He had been thinking deeply tonight, down in another, shadier tavern on the wharf, where in fact he had drunk abstemiously only a small portion of rough wine. It had seemed to him that, lust after Madame Croll as he did, yet there were plenty of other women in the world to fire his appetite. And Jeanne had become too difficult, and shrewish. Best get shot of her, as he would Luce. Damn them both. He would go travelling, leave the City behind. With enough money in his pocket he could have a jolly time. And then, who knew? A richer prettier *younger* wife might come his way. If you married once, then why not twice? Who would know, if he altered his name? It was not, after all, as if he and Luce had been joined in a church. God had not come into it, so where was the harm?

He took off his shoes, and raising the single lamp apparently left for him, went up the stairs as softly as he could. A practiced robber, when he wished to be quiet he was both professional and effective.

Perhaps he could bed down on the sofa in her parlour. Yes, that would be the best method, with no chance of rousing her if she was upstairs asleep. But the instant he reached the landing, Lucide spoke to him from within the room.

"Billy, I'm here. Come in."

She sounded oddly serene. What she said was neither a plea nor a command.

Abruptly, he felt driven by nervous curiosity. It might, (might it?), be wise to learn what had gone on in his absence. He should act a little angrily, he thought, He had been driven out of his home by two termagant women.

He stepped through the doorway. "Well? What in Hell's Furnace happened?"

The painted lamp and a few candles burned consolingly. Lucide sat on the sofa he had planned to utilise. She wore her nightgown, he saw, one of the plain ones, and a light shawl.

There was the scent of summer night in the room, and a subtle perfume.

They made a pleasant change from the pall of soup hanging about in the house, and which had unreasonably seemed to grow worse the farther he climbed away from the dining room.

"Come on, then, Luce. What did she do?"

"Who?" Lucide asked, lifting her face. "When?"

'In the name of Christ – *her* – *Jeanne Croll*, that's who. *Tonight.*'

Jeanne... Croll–? Do you mean one of those girls who used to work for me?"

"Who else? Are you *mad*?" (*Be wary*, he thought abruptly, *she's mad all right. Old Joséphe told you so.*) Aloud Billy said, in a lower tone, "That's it. *Jeanne.* She was coming here, to see you."

"Well, Gui, she hasn't been here. No one has. Bette's gone to help her mother. And I had a little nap. Only about an hour, a few minutes more. No one called – unless, of course, I missed her while I slept. I suppose she's after her old job, but she can't have it. I think she steals things."

Thank Christ, he thought. Jeanne must have pulled herself together. So that was one madwoman less to deal with. Just deal with this one, now.

He paused for a moment then, and gave Lucide a long, puzzled look. She had done something to herself, he mused, other than put on scent. Her hair – he had never seen her hair like that. It was impressive hair. It would be worth her while, Billy concluded, to cut it off and wear a wig instead, because hair as good as that could be sold for quite a lot of money. And it was wasted on Luce.

Although... although she truly did have a different look to her. And her eyes – they were darker, surely – something about the lamplight? And her mouth, full and red –

"What scratched your face?" he asked.

"Oh that. I must have caught my cheek as I slept, a pin or something dropped from my hat. It isn't too bad. When I washed, I saw to it." And then she stood up, and the grace of her movement, fluid, almost animal, catlike perhaps, arrested him again. What went on?

"Now, Gui, darling, I know this is our special night, and I've had a little sleep, so I'm fresh and awake now. And see what I've got for you–"

Billy looked. There on the sofa, formerly hidden by Lucide, was a paper packet, open at one side to reveal the edges of a considerable amount of monetary notes.

Immediately, nearly instinctively, Billy moved to take hold of it.

But she was there in his way, so suddenly his body met hers. And she was soft and firm at once, cool and warm at once, and the scent of her rose in a pale, succulent mist.

She had taken his right hand in both of hers. She caressed it slowly, sensually.

To his amazement he felt his body answer her touch. He must be going as cracked as she was.

But, "Not yet for the money, darling. It's all there, waiting for you, it's yours, Gui, my lovely boy. But first, be nice to me, won't you? It's our special night, Gui, and I've waited so long for you, haven't I?" And she kissed his hand, and went on kissing, sometimes tasting him, too, his palm and fingers, with flame-like quick pointings of her tongue. "Look at me, Gui–"

"I'm looking at you–" And he was.

"I'm to be your wife now, darling. I'm yours. Oh, Gui, I love you so much, from the first moment I loved you. You're so handsome, so wonderful, and I'm not so bad, really, am I?"

"No..."

"Do you like my hair this way? Only you will ever see it like this. And–" she was unbuttoning the bodice of the nightdress– "only you will see my body. Look, here I am. My body that yearns so for yours. I'm a little older than you, but I feel young, Gui, when I'm with you, darling. Every sou I've got can be yours. Every sou. But let me live, darling. Let me be young with you. Make love to me, Gui, and then you can have anything you want. Just this once, Gui. Only once. Please, please, make love to me, my darling–"

Billy choked. He found his free hand was on her breast. "Blow out the lights," he said harshly.

She smiled, and went to obey him. As she did this he shoved off his coat, and then she was there too, in the vague cloudy starlight through the half-drawn curtains. Her hands and her mouth were on him. He did not mind it now, the pressure urgent in him. She was a woman, what else? Why not? He pulled her close and kissed her mouth. The sofa would do for the bed. He dragged her down. She seemed to twist flexibly as a cat in his arms, or a snake.

Scene 3

Dawn enters the City, slips along its hills, fills up its valleys and alleys. The Cathedral, far off as space, glitters like a diamond crown. At the black loops of the river, dawn bends down to drink, and its reflection lights the water into wine and deep blue ink. An artist, the dawn. What a gift.

In Lucide's parlour, where the early light seeps through the curtains' gap, and already it is growing hot, Lucide lies asleep on the sofa, and Billy sits beside her, watching her. He has sat like this some minutes.

Then, with great caution he gets up, watching Lucide all the while. He lifts the packet of money from the floor where it has fallen, places it on a table, and begins to put on those clothes he shed. All the time his watchful eyes never leave Lucide. At one juncture he freezes into immobility, when she shifts a little and sighs. But when again she is still he hurries on with his dressing. That finished, he picks up his shoes, and the packet, and goes to the parlour door and through it, without a single alerting sound.

He knows the worthless Bette will not arrive for another hour at least, even if she bothers to make an appearance. There are no worries there.

Billy risks putting on his shoes. Then he checks the packet. It seems satisfactory. Certainly it is more money than he has ever set hands on – without having to share it with other gang members.

He puts his head back around the parlour door. A last squint at her, and she is still sleeping.

She looks like nothing now, partly naked, rumpled and dumpy, her hair in tangles. What had he seen in her last night?

It was like some spell she cast on him – but such stuff was untrue. No, he had missed having Jeanne, that was it. And if you were really famished, you would eat anything, however sparse or stale. (Like that soup – the stink is everywhere, and in the heat increasingly foul – rotten almost. If he had eaten any of it, he resentfully thinks, it might have poisoned him.)

Presently, and continuing to move with admirably practiced stealth, Billy ascends the next flight of stairs to the bedroom.

He stops at the bedroom door for a moment, listening to the silent house. (The soup-stink is somehow even worse here.) Then he goes into the room. The curtains are drawn over, it is dark. He swings one curtain back and the day streams in. He walks directly to the armoire, only half noticing a shadow or stain that lies there, along the carpet. Stains have no interest for Billy.

He is intent on his goal. With patient, virtually noiseless aplomb, he opens both the closet doors.

From inside the closet, staring up at him, are the dead broken-green-glass eyes of Jeanne Croll. She is crushed up very small, as if she had been folded like a sheet, as if she is quite boneless. Her ruined red-black face is balanced at an awkward angle on her shoulders, framed in a static wire of hair.

Billy gives a gagging grunt. He staggers around, away from the corpse, reaches the door and rushes straight down the staircase, down all the way, past each landing, not troubling any more about the din he is making. Reaching the front door, which no one had bolted, he flings it open and erupts out into the street, leaping the steps, and crashing the door closed behind him as he goes, with a tremendous concussion.

Above, the noise wakes Lucide.

She sits straight upright on the sofa, looking frightened. But after a second or so, relaxes. Her face breaks into a gentle rather beautiful smile. She leans forward and touches the area of the couch where Billy has slept beside her. She strokes the fabric. "Oh, my darling Gui. My wonderful, wonderful lover." Then she leaves the sofa, and modestly adjusts the nightgown, adding her shawl.

Walking as if the stairs are made of golden glass, Lucide glides up the house to the bedroom.

Goodness, what had they been at, making love down in the parlour, not able to wait. Improper, too, but no matter. Today was her Wedding Day, and that would put all to rights. Her whole life she had waited for this. To be loved. To be loved was Heaven-on-Earth.

Going into the bedroom, where the curtain is wide and the closet doors stand open, Lucide notices Jeanne.

Lucide: "Martice! Oh, you do look stupid sitting there. If only your six disciples could see you now, though I suppose they're not much better off, either. But you're useless without them, aren't you? And what do you think of *me* now? I shan't be Mademoiselle Veilleur for much longer, you know. Today I'll become Madame Milait."

Lucide goes to the mirror.

"And my husband thinks I'm nice. If you could have seen us together, you'd have had no doubts. He loves me. He thinks me desirable. He doesn't think I'm too old for him. If only you'd seen – but you *can't*. It's private, what happens between a man and his wife. It's not for a bitch like you to know, let alone see."

Lucide looks over her shoulder at the staring remains

of Jeanne.

"So you'll have to take my word for it. None of you thought I'd ever marry, did you? Not Papa. Not even Joséphe. As for Grete – well. Need I say. And I *am* marrying. I'm marrying this morning. This is my Wedding Day. But you're lucky, there. You'll see my wedding gown."

Reaching into the armoire to come at the clothes post is rather awkward now, with the muddled bloody noxious heap of Jeanne crunched up there in the way. And there is blood splashed on various garments. Hopefully not on the gown.

"I trust you haven't made my dress dirty, Martice. That would be like you, to try to spoil it. But it's right at the back, it should be safe. I couldn't just hang it up like those other rubbishy dresses. Not a gown like this."

Finding it impossible to get past the spoiler, Martice-Jeanne, Lucide abruptly pulls the body out of the closet. It cascades to the floor like... a broken doll. Then Lucide is able to reach the yellow gown.

"Summer Tulip is the name of this colour. And no, not a speck of mess on it. Another failure, Martice, for *you*."

When she has dislodged the gown, Lucide throws off her nightwear and begins to dress herself. Without the assistance of Bette, it takes a little while to complete the dressing, but eventually Lucide has managed. Then she turns back to Jeanne on the floor.

Lucide: "Now then, is this proof? Even you have to admit it favours me, this colour. Oh, but I forgot, you can't see it properly, can you? Not without your nippers on. Just a minute."

Holding the skirt of the yellow gown protectively back from the corpse, Lucide rummages through the blood-stiff huddle of Jeanne's garments. She finds Jeanne's spectacles with fortuitous speed. She thrusts them on the mutilated face, and squeezes them home on what is left of Jeanne's nose. One of the lenses is cracked in several places. It uncannily matches the smashed appearance of the green eyes.

"There. That's better. Now you can see I'm right. It's a lovely gown, and not too young for me. Gui liked it. Do you know, he thinks Grete looks old enough to be my grandmother – though there's only six years between us. But that shows what he thinks of me."

Then she takes up her yellow hat and pins it on over her loose hair, in front of the mirror, smiling, turning this way and that, to absorb the effect.

Lastly, from the dressing-table, Lucide picks up the roses she left there in the water glass. All their petals have fallen. Only the stalks, the mummified inner insectile husks are left. But she keeps them in her hand: her wedding bouquet.

Outside on the avenue, a sound of running feet.

Lucide gives no attention to this. The only sound she is waiting for is that of the hired carriage arriving.

But then the front door crashes open as, not so long before, it had been crashed shut.

Lucide, forgetting the useless Martice-Jeanne, goes to the banister and looks over. From there, completely collected, and smiling, Lucide observes as Billy climbs up the stairs, in company with two policemen.

"Now Gui, dearest, why are these men here? You haven't done anything wrong, have you?"

Billy Milait was dough-faced, and his hands shook. But he spoke to her levelly.

"No, that's all fine, Lucide. These gentlemen just need you to go with them for a while, somewhere quiet, you see."

As he said this, both police were staring past Lucide at the thing propped by the armoire. Billy though had positioned himself to one side, where he could not see into the bedroom at all.

"But why is that, Gui? Heavens, it sounds very serious – and today – I *can't* today, can I, Gui – our Wedding Day – what is it they want?"

"Madame – er, mademoiselle," said the taller of the policemen, well-primed on what to expect, "there's no need to be alarmed. There's been an attempt to break in at your grocery shop. Nothing damaged, but we need you to verify a couple of facts."

Lucide's face slackened into the happy, almost mindless smile.

"Oh, that wretched shop. Papa forced me into all that. Said I must be responsible for myself in something – whatever that meant. I don't care about the silly grocers. But of course I'll help you. And after today I'll never go there again. I'll just stay with my handsome husband, and look after him, the way a wife should. Oh Gui," she added, turning now her radiant lunatic's face to him, "I'll be a good wife to you. You'll never regret you married your Lucide."

The taller policeman nodded rather severely at Billy, who like many villains was always acquiescent with any human exponent of the law.

Billy took Lucide by the arm.

"Not so roughly, my beautiful Gui," she laughingly protested. "No hurry. We have forever now."

Yet she allowed her beloved to lead her trustingly

down the stairs and out of the front door into the brightness of the morning, where the sunlight flashed in silky ribbons on the tall pitted pillars and the undone rusty cages, and the living birds that fluted through the tarnished summer trees.

A black shape was drawing near along the roadway. It had a look of a plague-cart from ancient centuries, or maybe of the mythic barge of Death, which bore an ejected soul away down the river, below ground.

But Lucide was only happy.

"What a lovely day," she told the shorter of the policemen. And then, suddenly pressing herself to Billy, she raised the bunch of dead rose stalks. "Here you are, Gui, my darling, keep my flowers with my love. Take care. Till our next meeting, my dearest. I won't be long."

Final Scene

Lucide Milait was considered to be insane, but her crime, especially since enacted by a woman, was deemed so heinous, so savage, (the victim had been pregnant, too), it was thought unavoidable she must die. If for no other reason than as a valuable lesson to other maltreated wives.

(There were, here and there, a handful of uneasy memories stirred by the trial. For had there not been another grotesque murder, similar to this one, some thirty years before? Never solved, then. Thank God, on the present occasion, the culprit was taken, and would be expunged.)

She was executed in the early autumn, in the old prison west of the City, known as the Dove-Cote.

On the hour of the execution, (which was at seven in the evening), a man now calling himself Gui Lebrun was seated in a public carriage, travelling north but just then drawn up at an inn. Though he was not without funds, a court intervention, lodged on behalf of the murderess's brother, had robbed him of most of what he might have anticipated – not to add what he, unwisely, had left lying in the house after finding the corpse of his mistress in an armoire. Truth to tell, he had been somewhat preoccupied at that time too, hiding himself from any incursion by the dead mistress's husband, Antoine Croll.

Gui (Billy) had grown a beard and moustache as part of such precautions, and besides was not really the man he had been. If any had thought to recognise him since, no one on this evening made the quaint deduction. He journeyed in peace. Or in what peace he could get. But after all, it was not too much in arrears, for Gui-Billy lacked imagination, just as he was mostly devoid of empathy. The flood of horror was already running off him and would, left to him, never be able to linger as an omnipresent penance. He was intent on a fresh life in another country. The public conveyance, now static, was due to halt for two hours at the inn, about one hundred and fifty miles from Marcheval, so that passengers might restore themselves.

Gui-Billy was looking forward to stretching his legs, having a drink or two, and dining.

He did, inevitably – half Marcheval did – know the hour at which Lucide's execution was fixed.

Getting out of the vehicle in the inn yard, the dusk already down and the auburn chestnut woods already black, he heard a clock strike. In tone it was not unlike the clock above the Aviary Market. Seven.

Well, then. It was over. Damned bitch. And it was, was it not, a blessed release for her. Life had been Lucide's cage, even he could see that. Now the door burst wide and out she flew, like one of the non-existent ghost birds on the bloody avenue.

Billy was about to walk into the inn, when an urge of nature, not incompatible with a long journey, instead sent him to the latrines.

Emerging from their portals some ten minutes later, Billy was alone in the yard.

Not twenty -eight steps off the lighted inn beckoned with its clink of eating implements and bottles.

But the other way the woods and hills were looming black against a clear indigo sky netted with rhinestone stars. And then, an unusual shift in the air, as if a cage opened in Heaven.

He thought, Billy Milait, a bat flitted over.

But next moment something had hold of him that was both much bigger and much more vigorous. In colour it was silver, with a hint of rose red. In shape, he partly saw, it was like a large flying snake, scaled like a fish, wide-winged, and with tendrilous, luminous hair. A face of sublime female beauty smiled into his. This was not the smile of a love-smitten woman, or of a lunatic, however. This was the delighted countenance of a dedicated predator.

There was no time, and swiftly no energy, to cry aloud. The creature had snapped all his bones, and every vertebrae of his spine, in seven seconds. It ripped out his tongue, his hair and beard, and tore up his eyes like gems from a sump. It left him suffocated, speechless, blinded, ruined, and slowly expiring in a pain beyond thought, able only to squeak. He died in seven minutes. But they were the longest of his life.

Of course this was unfairly horrible for those that found his cadaver. But quite the reverse for the creature that had formerly lived within Lucide, and which coma had given freedom – coma, or unjust, legal, physical death.

Note of Acknowledgement

The story 'Not Stopping At Heaven' is respectfully and gratefully dedicated to the late Bernard Lee, my Father, who is virtually its co-author, since the work is based very closely on his play of the same name, and employs not only the play's main characters and structure, but also passages of dialogue and direction, some in 'translated' form, and some verbatim.

Tanith Lee 2011

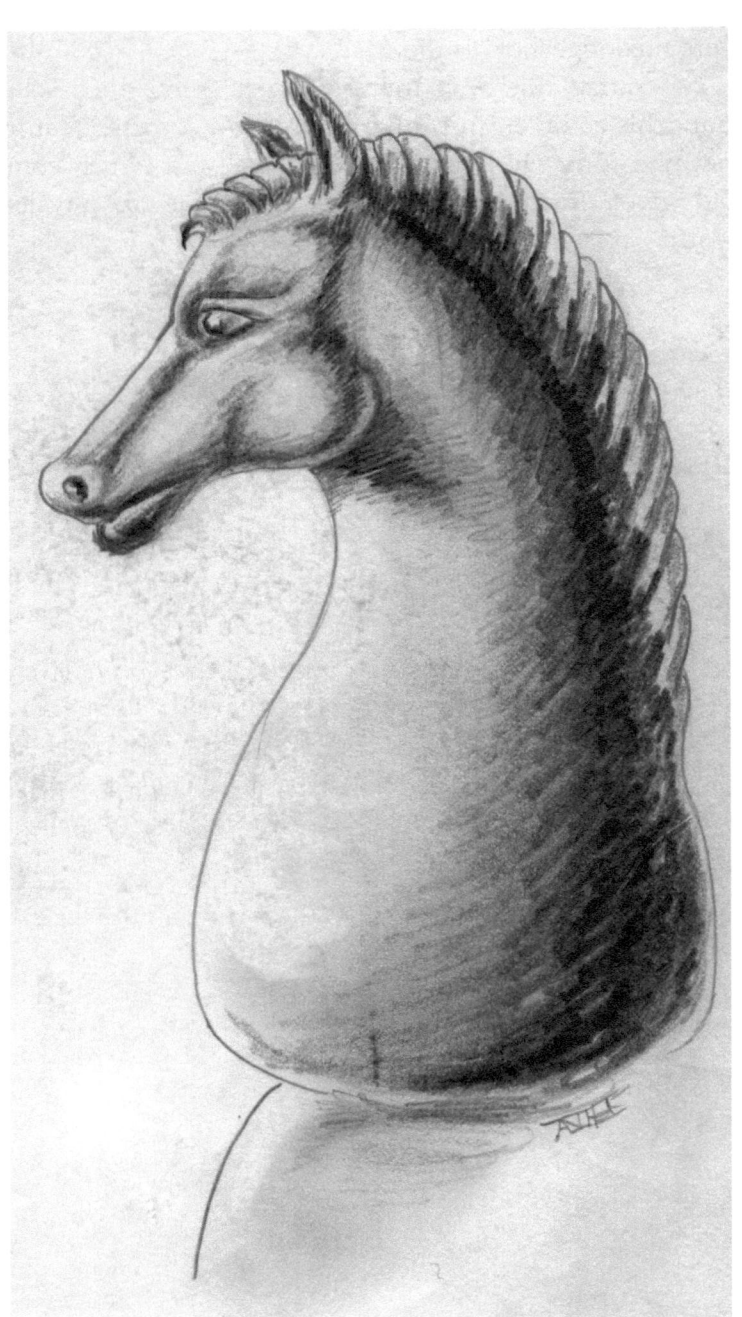

IDOLL

Chapter One

I, Dolfi, was brought to the Horrible House, in a covered carriage with two horses, (of which I was frightened), when I was six years old.

To this hour I recall how dark the street was, though the street-lamps smouldered a sulphurous thundery bluish-red. Where *I* had come from, we had no such lamps. But then, we had had nothing, and from this Nothing my father had died. While my mother, finding she could now become a successful whore, had 'given me up' to relatives. They it was who owned and lived in the House Horrible – as I have always called it, at least to myself.

Out of the exhausting and bumpily jumbling carriage I was pushed and pulled, over the uneven pavement, under the coal-black lid of an architectural city's winter night, and the smoulder-eyes of the terrifying lamps I did not understand, and across a paved court and up stone stairs and in at a tall, tall pillared doorway, like the portal of a mausoleum, I almost thought, having seen a graveyard at the age of four. Then in a buzz of sudden brightness, I was among them. My kindred, the Family de Raviret.

I was so drained and tired, made so idiotic by everything that had happened, the journey to the house not the least of this, that I stood there in a weightless half-conscious trance. Naturally, I could not miss their beauty, these shining creatures of alabaster and jet and copper, ruby, sapphire, purple, velvet and silk, who passed before me. Not for an instant did they seem real to me. As their name demanded, (my name was not theirs), I was viciously stolen, and ravished and enraptured by them on sight. They were demon-spirits. I had reached some hellish heaven.

I think I must have fallen down on the floor. Of that first meeting I remember nothing else.

Chapter Two

My original name, that is when I had been a child of the wild slums about the estuary harbour, the Bord, was Dolcefina, which means something *sweet* and *fine*. My father was an Italian, a sailor and vagabond. He named me, it seems, and also extended to me his own surname, Geli, as he had to my mother, so that she had ceased to be a Raviret. Along with all that, my father apparently had a mastery of the violin. His was an untrained, instinctual talent, yet he played 'like an angel'. I recall that being said of him after his death, by various acquaintances in the slum. He died of a fever, (but mostly of poverty), when I was almost five.

I have the vaguest memory of him. A faceless – for I cannot recapture his face – yet handsome man, with black curling hair and eyes of indigo. I was nothing like him, being pale-haired and -eyed, and having no looks at all. My mother, though, who, when he died, was herself only just twenty, was red-haired, and *her* eyes were amber. She had met also, and for two years by then been *attending* – as they say – an older and richer man. After a few months had passed over the violinist's death, this old wretch promised my mother she should have her own little house, with a servant and garden, and everything to make her life delicious. But she must give me up. He did not want a ragamuffin's daughter cluttering up his visits.

My mother did not argue. She agreed gladly. I myself witnessed this, and also I have heard the de Ravirets mention it in my hearing, with a viperish and quite false 'discretion', making sure in fact I caught the words. But it was true. She took no interest in me, and never had. I had simply been a trouble that befell her, and which now might be sloughed from her life since her paramour would pay my passage to the Family home, the House Horrible, in the City of Marcheval. And he would settle on me a small grant with increment, enough to make me less of a burden later when, the money having accumulated, it would be mine when I was eighteen. After which the grant would cease.

Because I had been taught to read, (I must guess by my father) I had managed, even by five years of age, to consume quite an amount of scurrilously sensational literature, (cheap paper books of this sort were not uncommon in the Bord, though mainly purchased by outsiders who could read as well as I). Therefore I imagined the Ravirets would murder me on the evening of my eighteenth birthday, as I would then be worthless. But at six, and some while after, this prospect looked a long way off.

Besides, I hardly knew what went on. Many and various things had made me both a stupid and a cunning child, timid and malevolent in equal measure.

There then we have the two editions of us: the exquisite Family in the Horrible House, and the Horrible Child allotted to them. The child which fell on the floor in a faint from mere enervation: Dolcefina Dolfi Geli de Raviret.

Chapter Three

The first years passed slowly. They might as well have been all one year, perhaps, equipped not with four, but sixteen seasons, each bout in four sets. To a child, or many children, I think, life is all a mysterious amazement, or a mysterious nightmare. Or both. Mine was this combination, and had been from the beginning, even those parts of it I had, in my conscious mind, already forgotten.

In the House I was taught to be washed, brushed, clothed, and fed at very regular intervals. (This had not been the situation, needless to relate, in the slums.) I liked, and disliked them, too, the novel regularities and the strictures – *how* clean I must be, *how* brushed, *how* neatly clad or fully fed – or restrained from over-indulgence. I was docile and obedient out of unease, and a soft, omnipresent fear. This fear also sometimes erupted into panic. As when the Lord of the House, Monsieur de Raviret, presided at a meal I must attend, (often I ate alone and escaped such worrying grandeur as occurred at the Sunday Luncheon, or the festival fare of their birthday celebrations). When sufficiently scared I could not eat at all. This earned reprimands from the Lord Raviret's second-in-command, his son, Monsieur Clément, and later from others.

One of my times of maximum terror, however, was when we visited the Cathedral, which perched so ridiculously high above the City. Luckily they, therefore I, did not jointly go there very often. But at Christmas, naturally, Easter, and other such fetes or observances as the Feast of St Agathe, or the Lamentum of Tears, we must call *en masse*, then sit out three or four hours of loud and echoing religious song, incomprehensible – to me – yet often alarming, with readings and lectures, dazzled and cloyed throughout by millions of candles and gales of incense.

But I was, as a small child, given to fainting. Or, presently, to the *pretence* of fainting. By the age of eight, when I had perfected this method, I was quite frequently spared the Cathedral, at least, as I caused all of them, particularly Madame de Raviret, and her personal maid, such inconvenience.

I had better describe the Family more thoroughly now.

Foremost there was Monsieur de Raviret (I never, as a child, learned his first name. Everyone in the place called him, publically at any rate, only *Monsieur* – as apparently the king's brother in the capital was called, prior to the Revolution). Madame though had a name, which sometimes was heard when – not her husband, but her son – playfully called her by it: Claudinelle. Aside from this trio there was another trio, the daughters, named in sequence from eldest to youngest: Aramine, Blaisette, Edvige.

And now, having named them, I will briefly list their looks. All were glamorous, as already I have intimated. Not simply their grooming and the richness of their garments and hairdressing. No, they were flawless... virtually flawless? To me, from the initial moment nearly until this one, they were gorgeous in beauty and physical grace. The ugliness inevitably lay, and lies, hidden within. Yet such visual power pervaded them that even as you saw them give some poisonous if metaphorical *bite*, you could not fault a thing. It was staggering. Those hundreds of nips and blows made worse, nearly insane, by their compensating camouflage.

Of the siblings, Aramine was the most senior at twenty. She was tall and slender, her eyes like sapphires, and crowned with raven hair. Blaisette, eighteen, nearly as tall, equally slender, was sea-blue of eye, with hair like rosehip honey. Edvige, sixteen, was nearly as tall as Blaisette, a touch more voluptuous, her eyes like turquoise, and with coppery golden hair. The son, Clément, was nineteen years of age, and his hair was a chestnut colour, just sombre enough, bright enough, to look both commanding and dramatic. He had steely hazel eyes, like his flame-haired mother. (Oh, yes, my mother's colouring had come from that side of the Family.)

There then they all stood, and stand, garbed in their wonderful clothing and expensive jewels. Unforgettable exponents of some ancient creed that states, it seems, the crassly wicked must be beautiful. Or is it actually the other way about?

Chapter Four

I was frightened of horses, as noted.

And for that reason as well I was afraid of the whole City of Marcheval, and most of all of the Cathedral.

Not everyone knows, in this day and age, the derivation of the City's name. Since, along with so many other 'gifts', the Family lavished on me a tutor or two, I was duly instructed in the City's history. (Although I had heard some of the stories, albeit in garbled form, from my earliest years. I do not even know who told these first tales, but scare me they did, for sure.) During my commencing nights in the House, once my exhaustion had been alleviated, I would often lie awake, listening in dread for a special and ghastly sound: the neighing of a demonic horse.

The City was begun, as so many cities were, by the Romans, when they spread their Empire, like a heartless golden butter, far across Europe, and the border kingdoms of the East. Pre Rome, prehistoric Marcheval had an older name, to do with a goddess of the river and the miles-distant estuary-mouth. That name I fail to recall. But after due time had melted empiric butter with the salt of uprisings, wars and greeds, the resultant metropolis gained a new title. This first civic name meant *The Saddle of the Horse of Mars*. (I do not know either the narrative of this legend, have never bothered with it.) But the Roman name evolved. *Le Cheval de Mars*. Mars' Horse. Marcheval.

Consecutively this horse of the scarlet Roman war god is a battle-animal. And so, it became associated, during the Christian era, with the Second Horseman of the Apocalypse. None of that, needless to recount, did I, as an infant, ever take in.

Nor even during my schooling. No, rather I absorbed the myth, the *mensonge noir* of a Devil Horse haunting the Cathedral roofs.

The Cathedral too has another name. It is *Our Fair Lady of Marcheval*. As with most such temples, the words connect it to the Virgin. Despite this, so the 'dark lie' has it, on occasion the pagan Devil Horse alights from some other, Satanic dimension, a red and fiery creature, glowing like a bonfire between the stony gargoyles that crane out from the towers. When present it is visible for miles, and casts down a burning light, as if the City itself had been set ablaze. It neighs, the Horse, its raucous challenge, but whatever that challenge might be – who knows? Surely, not anything *good*. There was too, sometimes, a rider on its back. The gender of this being is not stipulated. Mars, war-personified Himself? Or something even worse...

My earliest dreams were stalked by this phantom steed. (Even the sight of a chess-piece – a knight, with horse's head – appalled me.) Just as my early days in the City were marshalled and coerced by the Family.

I was, or my *mother* was from some cousined off-shoot of the Ravirets. This the only reason they took me in. The increment would have been nothing, or so I thought in my dawning womanhood. As I could in childhood speak a little Italian, they had told me I might, due to the education they lavished on me, have a chance as a 'governess'. (I did not, in fact, know what a 'governess' was.) But as time ebbed away with the tides of the City river, I lost my Italian, or it me. Only the most irrelevant or fatal words remained to me after the age of nine. Sweet... fine... *diventare orfano*.

Chapter Five

My rooms were small, although at twelve I was given a slightly bigger apartment on the third floor. I see no point in detailing it. I slept and often ate there, did the tasks I was granted – study, ladylike chores, performed to the best of my bored and avoiding ability. I see no necessity either to enlarge upon the House. It was deducibly sumptuous and polished and lovely, with cruelty always at the surface – dead insects, animals and birds killed for the purpose of being exhibited, their glass eyes – on pins – glittering with fury and reproach. Also heirlooms looted from other lands; ornaments purchased by a kind of legal burglary to do with banking and inheritance. There were many servants kept to tend all this, and to cosset the Family. To these, I was less than the dust.

But there is one important thing, one further ritual event, which must now swiftly be presented to these pages.

It had to do with the Attic.

More, much more than that.

Immediately, and even without proper understanding, and at the age of ten – when at last they 'trusted' me (they said) to witness and partake in the rite – I came to grasp its daunting and absurdly immense significance. You could not miss it. Or, only some person emotionally and spiritually blind could have done so .

Beginning, at once I was afraid of it. Afraid of so much, Dolfi. What a coward you will think me. You would be right. Yet, in this one instance you too, or so I will hazard, might have been unnerved.

My birthdays were, along with the rest of the Family's,

always marked, mine by a very little festival, generally with the dreaded Monsieur presiding. I even received tokens, if hardly gifts, (a sewing-box, a book of the sayings of some virtuous matron).

On the evening of my tenth birthday, when I was very tired and wanted only to be let go up to bed, I was told that *now* I was senior enough, and might come with them to the top floor of the House Horrible. To the Attic.

I knew, had known since the first winter when I was six, that *something* went on in the Attic. The Family would go up there on those essential evenings, and now and then at other seemingly random times. *Very* occasionally one member of the Family might even ascend to the Attic alone.

At such junctures no clue was ever vouchsafed as to what could really be going on. They might, too, individually or as a whole, remain in the sloping rooms for several hours at a stretch. Or else return after less than thirty minutes. The servants, conversely, never appeared to venture so high.

Without deciphering any of this, nevertheless I had, in some opaque and childish way, still sensed the portentous. Not even our excursions to the Cathedral carried such compelling weight. Their going up to the Attic was in the category of a pilgrimage.

Chapter Six

The season was autumn, and all light had left the City, depositing a sort of afterglow of throbbingly fresh blackness.

Inside the House this hardly counted. Every room and almost every landing bloomed with lamps. Only on the last landing of all, a narrow and craning space, from which rose the final cranky Attic stair, illumination did not exist. Instead, Monsieur must strike a match, and wake up the solitary oil-lamp left on a table there.

No one spoke a word. They were abnormally hushed and stiff. Taking my cue, as I had had to learn to, I did as they did.

For *my* natal days they had never dressed up to any extra degree. Today they had. Even I had been told to put on my best, a drab little grayish frock suitable for an older female child. Up the last stair we quietly crept, (for they did *creep*, all their arrogance quiescent), and lordly Monsieur inserted, one after another, three keys in the locks of a thin wooden door that opened directly off the top step.

The area beyond was a gloomily liquid and pulsing black, just like the night over the street. More so. If any windows had ever existed in this Attic, they had been effectively smothered. There was a muted musk, like fading roses, stale wine – Monsieur went before us into the space, holding the lamp rather higher than his head. From my reading and study, his stance at once struck me as that of a priest who enters the Sanctum. He confirmed my opinion. He nodded deeply. No, he *bowed*, to something that was well beyond the edges of the door.

And an awful fright gripped me. I could hardly move. Had it not been for the sternly guiding hands of Aramine and Blaisette, I think I might have run away. (Disobedience, as a rule, earned slaps, or a beating.) I was suddenly too alarmed to begin crying. My dry eyes seemed to stand wide as my face.

All about me the Family had gathered into the Attic. Last to enter, smooth as a cat's paw, Clément shut close the door behind us – and, to my elevating fear, locked it again three times with the fateful keys.

Had I been younger of course I would have dropped senseless. But the years of pretending to it had taken their toll, and now the knack would not come. As for sham, I did not dare. Even I, the runt of the litter, knew fakery – *here* – had neither credentials, nor chance.

Chapter Seven

I shall never forget what I saw then, against the dark, and lit up by the lamp, when the Family again thrust me irrevocably forward. Had I had in those seconds a voice – and had I *lost* all my cunning – I would have shrieked. But my voice was gone, and my bestial slyness stayed. Silently I stood beneath the heavy shoulder-resting clasp of Monsieur.

"Now see," said Monsieur, coaxingly and fawningly, (not, evidently, to *me*), "here is our little rescued cousin, poor little Dolfi. Today she is ten, and so we thought it fitting to bring her to pay her respects. Kneel down, girl," he added in a brisk aside to me. And as I did this, I realised that all the pack of them were kneeling, in a wing-like rustle of female dresses, and the mild creak of Clément's newest shoes. Monsieur kneeled next and last, beside me. "There," he said to me, with condescending beneficence. "At last you can behold her. Our patroness. Our queen. Our *lady*."

I thought it dead, the thing that sat there on the satin chair .

Was it old? Was it an old woman? In the bronzen flicker of the lamp it had the appearance of something recreated from a tarnished oil-painting, perhaps of the Eighteenth Century. A modelled image, a *puppet* – with – it seemed – jointed skinny limbs, and a long and skinny *wooden* throat. It had been got up in a full-length dress that, to me, looked as near to black, and so to the blackness that pressed everywhere against the highlight of the lamp, as a vile new material woven out of shadows. High up in this grotesquery – less a puppet perhaps than an assembly of dressed bones, for it was fleshless, ungainly, a skeleton in a gown – were a *head*, a *face*. Skull-like, somewhat *bird*-like. A bird of prey that searched as well for carrion, and ripped and roistered over and on battlefields, or charnel houses. Horrible it truly was. Horrible as the House I had, instinctively, named for it.

No eyes, there were only sockets. No lips, only a sort of toothless *line*. Bizarrely it had a bony arching nose – the beak of the *bird*. And all about the mask of it, this travesty, hung a lank spool of what must be meant to be hair. It was dull as unwashed wool, and of a colour as yet uninvented; no colour. Nothingness.

Chapter Eight

My memories of this initiating event, beyond that point, have remained somewhat piecemeal. Unable to go out, yet some *part* of my consciousness must have determined to absent itself. And so how long we were all there, kneeling before the terrible thing, I cannot recollect. This, however, I *do* remember quite clearly: that after some further while Monsieur again directed me,

"Say it," he softly rasped.

Say what? Oh, it seemed I must repeat some nonsense he had already said, and I, cunning and stupid, had automatically memorised. "Blessings on you, marvellous lady," I obediently whispered, voiceless yet audible.

And apparently I had done all that was expected of me, and it must be we all got up and left the Attic, and the sprawlingly-seated puppet-skeleton. I have the dimmest picture, half illusion it looks in retrospect, of the lamplight shifting in broken brassy blades, and the dark slicing back to take up the Attic, and all the world it could get hold of, in its jaws.

After which I think I had gone to bed, and lay shaking in horror, until the faint of sleep flung me from awareness.

Throughout the following days and weeks I filed the unpleasant event far back in my brain. I was well used to, and clever at, such filing. Gradually too, in a manner that, at the time, did not strike me as unduly odd, I grew steadily less and less afraid and unsettled by what I had been shown, or even by the behaviour in the affair of my guardians. So then, a freakish, life-size specimen of a doll had been put into the Attic. And the freakish Family, (who I had always hated, though revoltingly ravished by their garish physical opulence), went up at intervals to kneel to it, to placate and praise it. (They asked things from it, too, as I would find during later sessions. They even made to it quite sumptuous offerings – chalices of silvery Champagne or crimson wine, hot-house fruit and flowers, sweets, such examples.) It was, as I would come to see, less a doll than an icon, an *idol*, to which they bowed down, hoping and anticipating favours – success in their dealings in business or the social round. Very likely, when each in private with the totem, for their romantic ventures – Clément liked actresses, the girls coveted husbands, Monsieur took mistresses, and it is possible Madame, here and there, had recourse to a lover or two. It presumably seemed to them that the Attic doll granted their prayers – or if not, only withheld awards as the gods sometimes did, to punish, or protect.

Where the doll had come from was never said. They never mentioned it anyway, save when they spoke directly to it.

But for myself, I came to terms with the – shall I say *enterprise*. Which was as well, because, as already indicated, after my tenth birthday I was always enlisted in the joint Family Attic worship. Though I still often evaded the Cathedral.

Chapter Nine

The years ground themselves away, going a little faster as I grew older. At twelve I became a woman, that is, my courses began, to my great dismay. It was not I had never learned that women were subject to this trouble; in the slum, to avoid any physical knowledge, however disgusting, would have been hard. Yet somehow I must have believed I might miss the curse of it. I was taught, coldly and harshly of course, (by Madame), how I must most delicately cope with my affliction. Soon after, being by now of age, I was weaned to longer skirts, and shown, inadequately, how to put up my pale and disconcerting hair. As I heard one of the maids remark, one of two or three who reluctantly, now and then, assisted me, and whom I mutually loathed, "She'll never be up to much. Too daft to work for her keep and too ugly to marry."

So, it was I who was the parasite. While the Family, to my mind, were of less worth than a horse turd on the road, for that at least could be dried and used to start a hearth fire. The Family's only gift to any other, surely, was the money they might spend, should they even deign to.

On me, you will guess, they spent little. By fourteen, some 'genteel' work was being found for me, since I could copy in a legible hand and make readable notes for others. The remuneration for this, 'the pittance', as Clément once referred to it, went straight to the Family. How not? I already owed them so much, and must be delighted to pay.

During and after my fifteenth year, I was told to appear at some of the Family dinners and receptions to which guests were invited. Then I must wear my 'best' dresses. These were all alike, white, yet somehow a white lacking any lustre. Very plain too, to match, I must assume, myself. Their poor relation, Little Dolfi. The rescued cousin, yet, by a hundred twists and turns, totally dissociate from the Family – despite, let it not be forgotten, now once more bearing the Family name. Maybe they hoped after all I might attract the mistily-sighted eye of some old bachelor, some lawyer or civic official without too bad an income, who would then take me off their hands, himself thereafter a loyally grateful agent for their commercial ventures. Did I ever explain, the de Ravirets were not post-Revolutionary aristocrats of any type, but only one more clan of the upper merchant class? If I never did, perhaps it has been obvious enough. Meanwhile, the Family also saw to it I was quite helpful to them myself in 'little' ways. I would trudge two miles, sometimes in pouring rain or settling snow, to change their library books, buy them chocolates or fancy breads. Such services were beneath the busy servants. Should visitors arrive with children, I would be put in charge of the latter, while Madame and her brood played cards and gossiped. (I did not and do not like children, though I was never cruel to them, despite wishing to be, as some of these visitor offspring were frequently rude, over-boisterous and spiteful.) At the parties to which I was summoned, in my mediocre best clothes, I had left in my care the least attractive and most enervating of the guests, who doubtless thought quite the same of me. Even the old lawyers came to take pains to avoid my company.

Nothing, it seemed, would ever alter. By seventeen I had been moulded to the life of the House and my place there. I must yearn for nothing. I did not.

Of them all, when in the shrine of the Attic, I asked for not one thing, either aloud or in my heart. Although I always accompanied the Family. And besides, from my twelfth year, the year of my womanhood, I had gone up there by myself, yes, up to the Attic, in sly and utter secrecy.

Chapter Ten

I could pick locks since the age, I suppose, of four. What else, given my upbringing in the Bord? Like reading, I simply knew how to do it, and do not recall who taught me. I suspect not my father, he of the black curls and indigo eyes, who played like an angel the violin. But, perhaps it *was* my father. I think my mother, certainly, would never have bothered to pass me the skill.

And so, once the *idea* of the holy mountain-top of the Attic, and the bone doll that sat there, gained proper hold on me and I had ceased to fear, I took the pin I kept for the purpose, and the small stolen paring knife, and ascended the stair in the depths of the night – I, the coward, no longer, in this one thing afraid – and after a mere three minutes, as I judge, I let myself in.

I had picked other locks of the House before, I confess.

Even of the nocturnal larder, once or twice, (owing to those denials of my 'over-indulgence' mentioned some while ago in this narrative). Remember, I did warn you of me: stupid and *cunning*. Timid and *malevolent*.

Why I went to the Attic was at first through a kind of curiosity, perhaps. Or so I perhaps deemed it, if I ever pondered what I did.

Once in the black room, the door closed. I would sit down on the floor. In the beginning I never lit the lamp, or even brought a candle from my own slender stock. The thing was, after a while, I came to see quite well in the dark. Then I discovered the two windows behind their heavy drapes. I would draw the drapes open for the duration of my visit. The first time I did that a full moon, deep yellow as a wild apple, and scores of gas-blue stars stood over the City. Their light flooded in, along with a low glim of the street lamps scattered inartistically up and down the humped backs of Marcheval.

I then returned to my sitting place, and gazed again at the doll, who was now better lit and from both sides. She seemed less untidy and much less grotesque than when the piecemeal hackery of Monsieur's lamp had struck her. I decided I had better speak. This was not, by now, any kind of fear, only a mercenary wisdom: Pay your respects, just in case.

"Beautiful and fair lady," I said, employing phrases generally lavished on the Virgin in the Cathedral, "I hope you won't mind me."

She seemed not to. Of course not. She was a monstrous, life-size, lifeless, abominable wooden doll.

Why did they worship her, though, the hard-snouted and ice-hearted de Raviret tribe? Did they, against all odds, believe she *did* assist them, benefited their household, sent good fortune to them individually and as a composite? Then... to me? Never. That was not what *I* could expect, nor, being to some extent a pragmatist, what I ever looked for. It is inexplicable in its way, therefore, my starting to seek her. Or, seen from the telescope's other end, it is *far* from inexplicable. It is − inevitable, and apt.

After my first foray (I remained in the Attic an hour, for I heard one of the nearer church clocks mark the time) I waited until the impulse came again, which was some three weeks later. After *that* I did not pay my respects upstairs for some months, aside from the ensemble attendances at Family feasts. Clearly none of the Family suspected my independent observances. How could she get in, after all, this worthless and rather witless and weak young girl? Who, incidentally, always carefully relocked the door each time by means of her pin and knife.

On my later Attic-ings, and having seen how the Family made their offerings by then, I stole small missable elements from the House and myself offered. Gusts of perfume from the scent decanters of Madame and her daughters, such slight subtractions they were never noticed. Or a tiny sweet or berry from a dining-table decoration, less food than gem. Having no jewellery, naturally, of my own, I nevertheless found here and there a dropped bead – once even a dropped *pearl*, worth probably even alone, some wads of cash. These items I hid in the skirts of the doll. The Family offerings anyway were laid out there and only tidied away very randomly. The room continually drizzled the smells of fresh and decaying fruits, spilt wine, oils, and so on. Amid the multitude, the miniature seeds of Dolfi's obeisance were safely concealed.

Chapter Eleven

My eighteenth birthday approached.

I had begun to dream of the moment when the accumulations of my mother's owner's 'grant with increment' came due for me.

Four days after my birthday, (three evenings after my birthday Attic-ing with the Family), a servant told me Monsieur would see me at seven o'clock in his private study.

Some rather unusual things had been happening, I must report, during the past year. I had not, then, properly considered them. I thought them quite silly, the aberrations of others, or simply of life. People to me were (and remain) remote, potentially dangerous, unknowable and quite unlovable. (After all, when was I ever taught how to know, let alone to *love*?) Nevertheless, I should recount a few instances, if only to dress the stage for the production that presently was put on.

At a Family dinner with guests, some young man, quite uncomely I thought him, (was he not?), began to act strangely with me, staring in my eyes, passing me a flower from the table decoration, trying to take my hand in a doorway. As I say, I dismissed the idiocy. But, later by about a month, another, older fellow, some quite wealthy lawyer, I believe, accosted me as the guests passed to another room for a formal show, a reading, I think it was. "Oh, why not stay with *me*, my girl," said this grizzled legal merchant, "all that tripe will bore you to death." But I evaded the fool, and went in to hear some ludicrous work or other that, frankly, he had judged better than he had me. There were a few more like moments. Finally, there arrived a night when a rather dramatic older gentleman, less unprepossessing, I recollect, led my surprised self into the conservatory, among the dinner-plate-leafed palms – which hid all view of the outside vistas of Marcheval, Saddle of the War God's Scarlet Horse, (for whose appalling neighs I no longer lay awake listening). But before the current lunatic could begin anything else with me, Monsieur himself strode in, iron-black and freeze-white in his evening clothes. "Now, Vaudon, I must ask you, sir, to rejoin your sister, who is fretting." And like the grimmest shepherd of the two most wicked sheep, the Lord of the House Horrible drove us smartly back into the communal salon. My would-be diverter had gone quite red in the face. I took it for a brandy-flush.

Such episodes were incomprehensible to me.

I was even, I confess, quite glad the awful Monsieur de Raviret had saved me from extra discomforts. Although it was a far shout from those evenings when less wanted guests had been foisted upon me, and I upon them. And I, as I see now, how stupid. Yet again, who taught me to be otherwise? I had yet to learn: the lesson would soon come.

Chapter Twelve

The clock in the upper hall, which was silenced after ten each night, struck seven. I was already poised by the door, uneasily waiting. Not till the chime had finished did I risk my life by knocking at Monsieur's study.

To my startlement, *he* opened the way and ushered me in, courteously smiling. (Ah, Dolfi, you poor simpleton!)

Having been told to sit, obedient as a dog I sat. The little padded velvet chair was some distance from the huge desk behind which this Master of our lives presided. That room. It was dark brown in colour, like the richest coffee, and filled by the most masculine and dominant images – a vast mahogany safe with steel locks, (could I have picked *those*, I wonder?), priceless carved chairs, blood-dark rugs from Persia, cigar-boxes like shrunken wood coffins, a painting of a Roman Triumph, complete with chained slaves, the recreated form of some ferocious dinosaur, the height of a man and set with real ivory fangs. The chocolate curtains had shut out the City. The stained oak door had closed away the House. There was no sound in the room, whose air was the azure breath of cigars. I could hear the urgent stamp of my heart. And he – he *smiled* at me.

"Now, Dolfi, you must try to be calm and listen. I know very well how you women are often upset by financial problems. But you know you can trust me, don't you? It is the matter of this small – how shall I say? – allowance, which this friend of your mother's–" he laid no stress on any of these tasteless euphemisms (*friend*, *mother*) "put by for you. Under my advice, the grant has maintained itself, though I must admit, Dolfi, at some little loss to myself – please, please do *not* become agitated." I had not moved a muscle, how could I? I sat like stone. "Rest assured, I have managed any inconvenience. The House of Raviret has been more than equal to the – shall I say *carelessness* – of others. All is well." He smiled, he *shone* upon me. "But seeing, as naturally you will, what I have had to put into the affair, I know you, of all people, dear gentle girl, will grasp that now I must take full possession of this resultant, if hardly lucrative, fund. By which I mean, dear Dolfi, these moneys have already passed directly to myself. They will benefit the entire Family. I am sure, my dear, you will see how reasonable that solution is."

Chapter Thirteen

I sat like stone, an obedient stone dog. I had been robbed. But what anyway had I hoped for from it, that elusive and delayed monetary prize, the size of which I had not ever known? *Surely* I could have expected not much from it. Perhaps just the niceness of not having to beg every personal necessity from Madame. And, where she proved reluctant– "Of course you must darn your gloves *again*, Dolfi. They will do till next spring" – *steal* what was required from some repository with a pickable lock. One wisp of yearning there had been. This now passed before me, glowing like a dying match: I might have bought myself chocolate, a handful of flowers, some grapes, and from these specialities taken a proper offering, actually *mine*, to the Doll of the Attic Mountain.

As I said not a word, however, (what could *I* have said?), Monsieur seemed vastly encouraged. What then had *he* feared, the villainous latrine, some *tantrum*?

His name, as he told me not long after, was Auguste. "You must call me, although of course only when we are alone, *Auguste*." What an honour! Did even Madame de Raviret possess such benign licence? But I go too fast. Before he named himself, Monsieur rose again from his desk, and towering over me and all things, even the dinosaur, (had it in fact been made an inch or so the shorter than the two of them by design?), stalked here and there about the room.

"There is, however, dear little Dolfi, one further matter. I have been for some time aware how negligently, and often unkindly, you are treated in this household. You may be astonished I have noted this." I was indeed.

Had he not been part of the unkind neglect? "I regret this Family is imperfect, despite my guidance. Not even my son is quite as I would have him. No, Clément has not turned out quite as I would have wished. But there. I shall attend to all that in due course. Meanwhile, your own case. My child, I think we will do better to set you up in a separate domicile. Some pleasant little apartment, say, near the Revolutionary Monument. Your own little nest, with no others to harass you. There's no need for you to be lonely there, either. I myself, as your benefactor, will, my dear girl, take in you a special and affectionate interest. We will soon come to know each other well, Dolfi. What do you say?"

I sat speechless. I must have looked my usual slow, ignorant and brainless self. He frowned then, fearing he might have to enlighten me more vulgarly. But no, in truth, I was already totally apprised of his plan. The stunned expression on my face was not foolish naivety but utter shocked awareness. After all, I had encountered, third person, such a scene once before.

My mother with her aged protector. Monsieur Auguste de Raviret wanted me for his whore.

Chapter Fourteen

My future, and my present life, began in those harried and disgusting moments, the worst for me of any, perhaps, in the House Horrible.

But even fools can be canny, and as I have already told you, I was one such.

I *knew*, whatever else I did not want or *could not* do, I must *not* fall foul of this filthy and vile and all-powerful master. He always, it had seemed to me, had his way. Strong and clever men took care with and had given in to him; as for women, what other recourse did they have.

"Monsieur," I stammered, lowering my eyes, trembling – that was real enough – "you are too – *kind* to me, Monsieur–"

Relieved that I *had* caught his repellent drift, or enough of it the rest could be organised, he was all smiles suddenly. "Now, now, my little one. When we are alone – what did I say? – it must be *Auguste*." And without another attempt to woo, he arrived beside me and lifting me up, pressed me to him, and my mouth to his red and hair-blackened maw.

I endured his kiss, which was intimate, without vomiting, *only* because I knew I did not *dare*. And then – oh wonderful abruptly-available trick – I pretended once more to faint. *Entirely* to faint – every part of me limp as something boneless, while stilling my breathing through sheer practice and cunning artistry. Like a corpse I lay in his clutches. And very luckily he was not one of that other type of creature, which likes that very thing the best. Hastily he placed me on a long chair, puffing to himself in bad-tempered unease, chafing my hands – then letting them go. "Dear Christ," I heard the monster mutter, "have I *killed* her? Of course, you damned idiot, sir," to himself, "she will be in love with you! It's all too much for her – In God's name, she doesn't stir – now what?"

Before he grew panicked, and did some other nastier restorative thing to me, I opened my eyes and gazed at him softly, swimmingly. He *knew* I loved him? Then I must love him. "Monsieur," I whispered, as again he leaned over me, his hot, alcoholic breath on my face, "I have – I have adored you from afar so long. Oh, I shall die of this joy!" (Not for nothing, then, those odious, melodramatic play-and-novel readings in the salon.)

"No, you must live and be *happy!*" he enthused, grossly sportive.

"Oh, Monsieur." (I would kill myself before I called him *Auguste*) "Oh, I am your slave, my lord," (wise Dolfi – he liked this better than 'Auguste', naturally). "But – I must ask a tiny moment – a day... or so. Simply in order to collect myself together – I am shattered! Take pity, my lord. I must have a little *time*. I'm not able to pass directly, Monsieur, from sadness to – to Heaven."

Such luck! He was, beneath his thick and cruel alligator skin, a sentimentalist. (Probably *he* had chosen those romantic readings.) He assured me he would give me two days to myself. He would not even speak to me in company, let alone – alone. And then he would find a method discretely to remove me from the House, and I should live a life of modest luxury, (at least he had the grace to admit to the 'modest'), and when we could, we should be happy. After which, he let me go. I went.

Chapter Fifteen

The autumn night was blackly overcast, and strangely still in the midst of a City not famous for its nocturnal placidity. The House was, other than at the landings, sable. As I climbed the midnight stairs, I sensed all the while curious *entities*, spirits of the darkness. This was not necessarily my fancy. It turns out, I had always been more aware than is normal of other aspects, adjacent states, and of those forces too that, for good or ill, merge in and out of what is called Reality.

I entered the Attic. I smelled the vibrant sweetness of new figs, and nearly stumbled over a basket of chocolate apples – Clément, I thought, must have visited earlier. There was his latest actress, who he hankered for and had so far failed to get.

I sat on the floor in my accustomed spot, not even bothering to draw back any of the drapes. I had nothing to offer, and had not purloined anything. Monsieur, despite his promise, might be watching me. He was out now, however, at some dinner near the law courts, which would doubtless last until three in the morning.

Did I grasp why I had entered the Attic, sought the sanctuary of the Doll – the idol? In some way I must assume I did. But given what must next befall me – *Monsieur* – all I felt was emptiness and sickened apprehension, and all I could do was sit on the floorboards, cold and lost, without a scheme in my mind.

Then it was as if something broke inside me. Like a glass vessel. And I began to cry. And then the crying stopped and I heard my voice come stealing out of me, quiet and desperate as a thief.

"I don't have anything to give you. I've never had anything of my own. So I can't give anything to you. I've never asked anything, though, of you. Who am *I* to ask? Who'd hear me? No one ever hears me, unless I say what they want. I can't say what you want – I don't *know* what it is. But I never asked for anything – I shall have to run away. It's the only remedy. But how – and where – and even then he may find me – Save me, save me," I murmured; I heard my own voice, so pale and still. "Save me."

Then I bowed my head and the dark was so deep it was as though the whole essence of the night had been poured into the Attic. Outside, beyond the drapes, the skies must be bright as day, since every atom of the dark had settled here.

A relaxation came with this. I felt my body melt from me. I had no body. I was – nothing. Never before had I – ever – ever – experienced such a warm and serene comfort as was in the nothing that now encompassed, enveloped and possessed and was me.

I did not sleep. I did not lose consciousness. I floated in the entity of Total Night, and was one with it, in bliss.

And then everything was altered.

The first that happened was that the whole Attic began to grow light. It was like a very swift yet steady sunrise. Colours of rose and peach filled the blackness in, and then out of the softly burning moltenness, shapes of all sorts started to evolve.

The effect was so smooth, so all-encompassing, one could not imagine that what one beheld was anything but a fact. Nor was anything insubstantial. These initial appearances were the most real objects I had ever seen.

And they were flawless.

No longer was I in an attic. Not even in a room. The ceilings hovered far above me, the height of several storeys; the walls expanded to far distances, and columns lifted between – violet marble, black metal, green crystal, and silk curtains fell down in the colours of rain and rainbows. There was the scent of some rare perfume. And of foliage and fruit – magenta and orange fruit that grew, for there were orchard trees also risen out of the floor, which was of some material like a calm and lucid pool, through which you could partly see down to gracile things that swam below, fish or water-snakes; how could I tell?

But all this was only the backdrop and the frame; there was something else to look at.

I looked, and saw. I believe at once I sensed that, though they had had beauty rub off on them from their visits to the Doll, (even I, it seemed, had benefitted from this), yet the *Family* were the dolls, in plain terms, the Family, and I, and maybe all the City, all humanity, ugly wooden dolls like parcels of bones, with string or wool for hair and only blots of void where their eyes should be, and not a living *soul* among them. For the Soul was here. It was She. *Her*. The Doll.

I swung myself about on the floor that was a sleeping lake, until I lay face down before her. I, who had cringed and fawned and fiddled and failed all my eighteen years, I now lay stretched out in sheer and ringing ecstasy, to which the state of mere joy must be like the squeak of a wheel against the singing of nightingales. And so I stayed, in love forever, before the God that lived at the Mountain-Top of the House.

Chapter Sixteen

Her House is infinite, and full of a thousand and more chambers, courts, gardens. From every high vista, whether a window or a gateway, you can see out into a different place, or a different *world* – all of which, one learns, is some era of the City of Marcheval, but seldom as I had known it. When desired, one descends to those altered streets, among the builded hills, the valleys, the coils of the river. She, and therefore I, walk through the Roman colonnades that have existed there, and – here – still do, and through the plague holes of Mediaeval warrens, the flowering of Renascence palaces, the tribulations of wars which have been and those, as I, Dolfi, must see it, yet to come. Through her peerless eyes I have stared at silver pods with outstretched wings, threading the nights of Marcheval with embroideries of fire and brimstone, while the City flames. I have seen peace, too, and a bridge constructed of amethyst lights, standing high above the Cathedral, while beings like angels were flying there... And I, as Hers, have ridden the scarlet Horse of Mars across the night sky – yes, even that. He wears no saddle at all What can ride such a mount *needs* no saddle, none.

Running into the attic I said to her I could give Her nothing. I said I had never, before, *asked* for anything, as I had not. But now, I said, I begged Her to salvage me. So She took me to Her, saving me, answering my prayer – and also accepting the only offering I could truly make; one combining contract. For what I asked from Her, and what I gave to Her, then and always was my own Self.

I now am part of Her, as are all the chosenly accepted

others. We exist with the supra-paradigm of what She is, physical yet not as 'physical' has ever been known to be; *incorporeal* – yet of the flesh. But it is the flesh of stars.

And, as a part of Her, safe forever, in love and loved *forever* , still I am myself, as all the others who serve and love, and are loved within Her, are. It is we who sustain Her earthly life. When we flow, like clear water, into her Paradise, we feed and fuel Her for Her continued presence on the earth of Man. The pleasure and sweetness this is, is beyond describing. The world has never had, nor ever can have, language capable of such descriptions.

As for what I was, that poor little orphan fool, she vanished from the house of the de Ravirets. They decided she had run away. Just as Monsieur de Raviret had originally intended to tell everyone, after he had installed her as his property in some slum near the Monument. Probably he was very angry. Such a shame.

With and within Her, we never notice who comes and goes to or from that attic that is, so strangely, the other side of the coin of this gleaming dimension where now we are. There are other such coin-sides, of course. Other attics, cellars, heights, depths that, given the correct awakening, will lead to this one. God knows what, where, We do not bother about them. Now and then some new soul comes in to join us. They are always rhapsodic, and welcomed, and fit inside our composite company, each like another matchless jewel in a necklace of infinite capacity. Our life, and our lives, now, are as eternal as is She.

What more is there to tell you, then?

Do not try to envy me my Happiness. You cannot even envisage it. It is beyond you. It is beyond the world. It is – Beyond..

The Portrait in Gray

Even things that are true can be proved.

Oscar Wilde

From his own preface to *The Picture of Dorian Gray*

Prologue

That English summer when Robert was five and Alice just eleven, he had confided in her that their governess was frightening him with tales of how the cook put the tongues, ears or noses of dead – or even live – persons into certain of her sauces and custards. Properly ground up, it seemed, these organic articles would be undetectable by anyone, save a connoisseur. Among which order, it transpired, the governess was numbered. Why she had begun this cruel prank against Robert he clearly did not know. But Alice herself, already a girl all eyes, suspected it to be because their father, the widower Sir William, had taken a gallop or two with the governess, and then dropped her for a tasty new barmaid at *The Fox*; Robert meanwhile, though so young, bore a strong resemblance to his handsome sire. Alice reassured her brother that the cook *never* made culinary use of any human body-part. And since not once had Alice lied to him, Robert grew calm, and stopped vomiting after almost every meal. Alice however was not quite done. During the following month she managed to insert, into various of the governess's meals, the tail of a dead shrew found in the gardens, a handful of shed snail shells, some potent laxative powders from the medicine chest, and two or three thin, long metal screws spotted on the floor of the church. The governess, in order of assault, screamed, choked and spat, spent an entire day in her closet of ease, and lastly broke a front tooth. Her resultant tirades postulated that either the children, or the cook, "had it in for her." Her ire went unattended, until finally recognised by Sir William's giving the governess the sack. The cook was a good one, and Sir William enjoyed his food. While the children, being his own, were naturally beyond reproach. About four years later, Alice found herself by chance on an omnibus with the former governess. Alice by then looked very different from her more childish self, but the governess was very much the same, and additionally identifiable from the gap in her teeth. Alice contrived to sit beside her. Presently, making pretence of waving away an insect, Alice drove a hairpin one full inch into the governess's arm. As she screeched and flailed, yet ignorant of Nemesis, Alice withdrew the pin seamlessly, and remarked, with mild concern, "These wasps are so terrible this autumn."

One

Several years in turn after that episode, which in the consciousness of Alice had already been reduced to a faintly wistful pantomime, Alice stood in the alien French City.

At this time she was twenty-three years of age. But more significantly she was still her own master, willingly unmarried, and quite at liberty.

Clever Alice.

She had other names.

For half a decade she had been established as rather a well-known watercolourist, a fashionable creatrix of both landscape and portraiture. If not in the league of such as Singer Sargent, she had attained – for a woman – great renown, and risen lucratively decently high.

Also, until the previous year, until the twentieth day of last year's December, she had been happy.

Caught up from about the age of twelve in the flaming desert of her intense creativity, Alice had even so kept one particular oasis. For although she flourished in the desert, where always she could lose herself, she needed too sometimes to get refuge from her own fire. Until that twentieth day in December, when she learned the oasis had been destroyed – its shade-giving palms burned to cinders, its wells poisoned.

Now, strolling or pausing on the broader streets of the alien metropolis, a perpetual shadow, quite unlike cool shade, gnawed inside her. She had no intention either of casting out this hungry serpent. She wanted its company; its composite pain and fury were all that were left of the charm and sweetness that had been before.

Reaching a terrace then, Alice Pender, (and her inner shadow), came to a halt and looked about.

She had been in the City four days, and had gradually come to the idea the architecture by the river metamorphosed. For example, one moment you might see the colossal, prehistoric-seeming, dinosaur-boned Cathedral crouched on its hill – and next, as from here – it had ethereally slenderised, putting out extra windows and towers. And the loops of the sea-tending river water, and its myriad bridges, changed direction. Yesterday one would swear that *particular* avenue had opened on that *particular* bridge... but today it seemed a mirror image, even back to front. Well, this river was the Styx, they said, from the classical Hell. Or Lethe, which you drank to forget enormous hurt.

Alice thought of an odd poem she had once read, whose author was forgotten. Its disembodied lines filed slowly through her brain.

> *Oh let me go down and find*
> *The waters of forgetful night,*
> *And drinking them underground,*
> *Unremember you quite.*
> *All memory take – your face, your name,*
> *Till nothing remains.*
> *But still my heart breaks:*
> *Lethe leaves me to grieve, though I*
> *No longer know why.*

A dreadful man, (she did dread him when he approached her), abruptly came to her side and began to harangue her in the French tongue. Though perfectly conversant with it, she feigned confusion. He wanted, urgently, to escort her, show her all the wondrous sights of the area which otherwise, she being only a foreigner, and a woman, she must miss. And after, perhaps, a little luncheon?

"Forgive me, monsieur," said Alice in deliberately unsure French, "my brother has just died."

She did not wear black, of course, and the dreadful man seemed not to believe her. But something in her face suddenly drove him back. He scowlingly nodded, and made off, as if having received his marching orders. Alice, as a rule, had been able to settle such matters since the age of fifteen.

She had her reason for being in this City. It had nothing to do with vaunted sights, or even artistic views, though she might well have said it did.

Moving along the terrace before the tall pillars of some bleak and obscure building, she stared across the leaden silver band of the cold spring river below. A house stood up on a hill opposite, groved round with bare trees. It was painted in a creamy veneer, but with crow-black shutters. Her destination. Her purpose.

An unexplained glitter surprisingly plaited through the river below.

Indeed, such water could *never* allow forgetfulness of any sort.

In a tall upper room of the house with black shutters, Eugenie Valotif sat choosing her gown for the evening. The maid was bringing from their covet all the most recent costly dresses.

But the slippery pastels and pigeon-dark velvets bored Eugenie. She had worn almost all of them once already.

"Stupid fool," she said in a lazy tone to the maid. "Look harder. Are you blind?" And as the girl hurriedly spun back to the covet, Eugenie flung at her the hard little bolster from the settee. It caught the maid behind one knee so she was unbalanced and nearly fell. Eugenie gave a disgusted laugh. What mortal dross I must put up with! it seemed to say. (The maid thought herself fortunate. There had been far worse).

Eugenie rose and went to a window, gazing out for a moment over the slanting clusters of roofs and the dirty platinum river, to something curiously winking back at her, some way up on the far bank.

How bizarre. Was it a pair of opera glasses that gave off, between those columns, that funny quick and splintery flash?

"How beautiful she is! More so even than they report. And her gown – Persian silk, wouldn't you think?"

"Very likely. And so effective, that sable with her white-blonde hair. Although she almost looks as if she's in mourning–"

"And well she might, my dear. That multitude of lovers of hers who have died, or *killed* themselves, apparently, because of the withdrawal of her regard."

"One threw himself beneath a train–"

"I heard another climbed into a lion cage at the Zoological Arbour in London, and was rent limb from limb–"

"Another jumped from a high tower in Rome–"

"What nonsense. No one does such things merely for love in these modern days. We have electric light now, and boned bacon."

Eugenie, the target of so many trills of gossip, had just now glided by to take her seat for a minute or two of music. She was indeed almost uncomfortably beautiful.

She seemed chiselled, both form and face, by some spirit genius, then cased not in skin, but a lucent white sheathe intended originally for some newly opened flower. Her marvellous hair outdid the lustre of the ravishing silk gown, (which had been sewn and trimmed for her at much expense, only that afternoon). What shade were her eyes? Could one say? They were too rare a colour to be listed on earth. Unnameable, perhaps Venusian – Her only other jewel was the eleven foot skein of milk-white pearls, that looked more sallow than her complexion, and which wound round and round her flawless neck, before trailing next almost down to her exquisite ankles, where each independent strand ended in a tiny diamond star.

Scarcely noted, a small orchestra had taken its station in the salon; a harp, a viola, a violin, some other constructs of string and shine. A famous singer was to regale the company. She had held them, at the Goddess of Music, spellbound. But knew that tonight she would hardly get a hearing. So things were in such sociable spots.

One of the older men at the perimeter of the room murmured to another, "Shall we slink out before the caterwauling starts? A smoke on the balcony would suit me better." And then when they were outside in the sharp spring chill of dusk, their hot cigars jeering at the icy stars above, the dull sentry-lines of street lamps stretching away, a thousand hilly windows blushing up, the first man added, "What do you think of her?"

"Oh, a stunner. Thank God I'm too old to be moved by all that. At my age it's like a flicker on a cold hearth. Was that a spark? No, been and gone." They laughed softly, as in the closed room the concert began, Vivaldi, the other man believed, while the chatter of the guests remorselessly continued above and beneath. "But men do die of her," this man said, only as if musing. "I heard of a fellow in England, not four months ago. He'd wanted to marry her. But she made a fool of him, told him she wouldn't have him if he were the last man alive, and this in front of witnesses. He walked out and hanged himself. Rich, and good-looking, it seems, and a title – Pen-Devon, that was it. Seventeen years of age." They sighed, (jealousy for seventeen, pity for death at seventeen), and the breeze of spring, a razor still not yet a caress, sighed with them more harshly, like a dragon in the budless garden trees.

The singer pitched a strident E. She was angry possibly at her boorish audience; the note was a sort of admonishing shriek.

The first man remarked, "That English girl is here too, the artist. Note, in the front row, and by God, she actually listens to the aria."

"Her work is very good," said the second man. "I have a landscape of hers. What's her name now? Ah yes, Alice Pender."

"I've heard she has another name, too," said his companion .

"What's that, then?"

"In English, a sort of pun. They call her – not Alice – but *M'alice*. It seems she also has done, or caused, some interesting things. But it may all be hearsay. Even the tale about that young fellow hanged himself. It may all be lies, like virtually everything else."

Eugenie only looked. The indescribably-coloured eyes fixed with a sort of haughty potential – if false – patience.

"Indeed," she said. "I've not heard of you,

mademoiselle."

The male host protested. "But Mademoiselle Pender is a celebrity – both in her own country and in Europe. Even here."

Alice smiled. She thanked him quietly. Turning again to Eugenie, she said, "But Mademoiselle Valotif can scarcely have had time to hear anything of that sort, let alone to know any of my work."

Something occurred in the peerless blonde face. It – *settled*, slightly. At this moment, maybe, an observer might deduce some being lurked within or behind the delicious exterior of Eugenie – that was unhuman.

"Is your painting very good, then?"

Alice nodded. "Yes. Good enough. But you see, I sometimes lack a challenge."

Their host leapt into the breach. Probably he felt the lash of indifference: both women were, to him, indifferent, and he could have no true part in any of their dialogue. "Mademoiselle Pender's work has been exhibited at several important London galleries – and even in the City, at the Clock House–"

Eugenie did not shrug. She might as well have done.

"Perhaps," Alice said softly, "I could invite mademoiselle to my little house here. The matter of half an hour."

"Why?" said Eugenie.

"You will see what I can do."

"Why should I require to?"

"Because, mademoiselle, you are so beautiful, yet so unlike any other beautiful thing, whether sentient or inanimate, that I want very much to paint you."

"Ah," said Eugenie. "And your fee is high, I must suppose."

"I would not ask you for a sou. I would ask for nothing."

"Then I must assume you're quite mad, mademoiselle."

Alice bowed. There was to her an essence now indefinably yet coolly masculine. "Here's my card. I leave the matter with you."

"Why," said Eugenie, not glancing at the card, "do you want to carry out this crazy act?"

"I've told you, mademoiselle."

"You've flattered me, mademoiselle. That tells not enough."

"Visit my studio, then," said Alice.

Her eyes had darkened to the mourning neither she nor Eugenie had put on. A snake gnawed Alice's heart. It had carved – bitten, warped – this heart into the form of an apple tree. And now from the heart-tree, she offered up an apple. *The* Apple, which was Knowledge of Self. Did Eugenie sense it? She only faintly smiled. And all around the noisy guests were laughing at this and that, while the frustrated soprano from the Goddess of Music cast out her final note. Sheer as steel it shot through the chandeliers, somehow not cracking them. And so unrecorded, as with everything which is not, it vanished into thin air.

Surely Eugenie did not – *could* not – register the import of that?

A day after her first visit to the cramped little house near the Academy, Eugenie Valotif sat there again, on a velvet couch, wearing an afternoon dress of palest gray, while Alice Pender sketched her. With what seemed to be the most carelessly bold strokes, as if – rather than *draw* her subject, the artist continually wiped some recurrent stickiness off the paper.

The easel of course faced the artist not the subject. Though a watercolourist, to use an easel was Alice's normal practice. Instead of a stretched canvas for oils, the paper block was crucified on a board. This way, therefore, only the motion of Alice's hands, body, eyes, was visible to any sitter. And *never* the evolution of either drawing or painting.

Alice had said at the start, "By accepting this you accept my terms. You may not look, mademoiselle. Not until everything is done. No client of mine is ever allowed to."

"Oh, why?" asked the languid Eugenie. She had seemed languid, ever since first crossing the threshold.

"Because, my dear and peerless mademoiselle, before it's finished it won't at all resemble you. It never does, I find. You must trust me."

"*Must* I?"

"At least, you must *obey* me." And at this Eugenie had laughed her superior and dismissing laugh. She, the goddess-queen, to *obey* such an underling. "Think of it," said Alice Pender gently, "as your game. The novelty, after all, will be worth a lot to you. Where else in your adult life have you had to *obey* a single person?"

"How do you know I have not?"

"It's written in your beautiful face, mademoiselle."

"Will this portrait then show that?"

"The portrait will show *you*, mademoiselle. That is what my art does, it seems. If I'm asked to paint a linden avenue, I paint the essence of every tree, the spectres of moonlight that have become tangled in it, the strands of sun, its historical psyche, every dream dreamed under those boughs. And with a human subject – the same. Day and darkness, sun and moon, the dream, the heart, the soul."

"So much? Your opinion of your talent is high."

"I say only what others have said, written, or told me. And I think anyway you've already learned that much."

As indeed Eugenie had.

She had had research done on the career and fame of Alice Pender, and all the information gathered she had bothered to scan. There was, even by then, quite an amount.

Alice had not been boasting. She had been quoting certain venerated critics, even a French critic, himself of vast renown.

If not fully satisfied, yet Eugenie seemed prepared to play this 'game'. It had credentials. No doubt even if she had not understood the message of that perfect finishing soprano note, some *atom* of her *had* grasped a meaning. *Let me not die.* Oh, she never would die, evidently. Eugenie was young and rich and gorgeous and healthy. Physical eternity lay before her. But even so. From our youth our own ghosts already live in us. Oblivious though we may be, sometimes they speak. Why else the mirror, the canvas, the photograph?

Two

There had been snow falling on the day she received the letter.

She had just come back to her rooms from a long shopping expedition, buying embroidered gloves, chocolates, and bottles of bright sherry for her Christmas gifts. Alice was cheerful. She liked the artistic contrast of her smiling fire and lamplight and the assembled presents only waiting to be wrapped, with the tombstone black and white of the elegant street outside. She stood at her window with a cup of tea, watching as one by one the glass of other windows began also to be poured full of bright sherry. And then her landlady knocked on the door: "Oh Miss Pender, this has just come for you." A slender envelope addressed in an unknown hand... some new commission perhaps, it might have to wait until the festival was over... She had been so careless of it that she set it first on the mantelpiece by the clock; she would read it tomorrow. But then she thought possibly it concerned some materials she had ordered at Stenhopes. And so took it down and opened it by the lamp, and read: 'With great sadness I have, I regret, to inform you of the death of your brother, Sir Robert Pen-Devon.' At which the street of tombstones and the pitiless pallor of the snow slid in at the window and covered up the room, and everything, in falling white and night.

He had been at the estate. At the huge old rambling house, in the west and near the sea, that very same house where, twelve years before, the governess had frightened him, and Alice had put paid both to the fear and the governess. This time Alice had not been with him, but in London. Yet if she had been there would she have been able to divert him from his course? It seemed unlikely. His – *plan* – had been so absolute. And he had already, surely, so much to retain him in the palace of life. Handsome, and with the security of money and position, and a circle of friends too who had liked, loved and admired him, and would mourn him bitterly, resentfully, for years to come.

There could be no doubt it was suicide. He had left a courteous and regretful note, apologising for any distress and inconvenience caused by his act. The note was not, either, filled with recrimination. It carried no recital of the agony which drove him out of existence. Let alone of the agony's instigator. Nor did it contain any clues to his whereabouts. The body went unfound for some days. He had taken care, it seemed, to go away into the deepest of the estate's woods, where winter-hungry foxes and birds might well have discovered him first and cleaned his corpse to the bones. But failing that, as rather strangely it did fail, only the tough labouring men who maintained the trees should accidentally have come on him. And since he had sent off early for a seasonal holiday, and with a liberal bonus, all the house staff, (saying he was to visit elsewhere for Christmas, which had happened before), the note itself should not have been found until the New Year. But the housekeeper had chanced to go back on an impulse of her own, and so found it.

Next the police entered the scene, and in the end the men and dogs, having scoured the many miles of the estate and surrounding countryside, confronted, in the cold-preserving snow, the black the tree and the thing which hung from it, like a broken bough, but it was

Robert. Alice's Robert. Her calm and inspirational refuge, the oasis, the one being she completely loved. As only sometimes a sister can love a brother, or a mother a son, or a daughter her father – a passionate and deeply rare love that, having nothing sexual or possessive in it, somehow transcends itself, and is another emotion for which, maybe, no true name was ever coined.

Robert's last letter to Alice, which later she judged had also been written in the hours before his death, had reached her five days ahead of the solicitor's envelope. She had read the letter on the fifteenth of December with (of course unsuspecting) pleasure. There *was* nothing suspicious in it. It referred to a few times of their childhood, but quite frequently they did write, or when together speak, of these times. It asked her ordinary if interested (had they been?) questions about herself and her own daily life. It seemed he wanted to meet her soon after Christmas. Afterwards, she tenaciously re-read it often, trying to determine if or how he had deceived her. It was a fact they had not met since the previous April. But absences happened, generally due to their individual pursuits. She had meant to reply, but various quite nice trivia delayed that. When she learned of his death, she was incredibly thankful she had *not* had space to reply to Robert, unknowing, after he had died on the black winter tree.

There were enormous crowds of people at his funeral. Robert had left all his wealth among his servants and friends, and assorted householders of the area. Even the estate he gave in shares among them. He and Alice had talked of this nearly frivolously long before. She did not need houses, land or money, nor did he leave her any. Nor anything, as it turned out. As if he perfectly comprehended, (what else) that to be given anything of his after what had occurred, would be like giving her a punishment, a *curse*.

Robert had once, very briefly, alluded to an acquaintance with a young French woman, Eugenie Valotif. In that letter, which preceded his last by some months, he made not much of it. But once or twice, clandestine as despair, the funeral guests had also muttered about the woman, always breaking off if Alice drew near. But she was all ears, as still she was all eyes.

With hindsight Alice realised that the slightness of Robert's written allusion to Eugenie indicated a sort of bashful reticence.

Had he thought Alice might be jealous after all? But he had, since his fifteenth year, had women. At seventeen she would have thought it odd if there had been no one to stir his romantic love, at least his animal lust. He was like their father, though much more fastidious, and more kind.

Steeped in the waters of her own life, she did not take enough notice, demonstrably, of the life of the angelic oasis. The premise had never assaulted her, esteeming him as she did, that even he might be polluted, ruined.

But when she put her mind to it, as immediately she did, she had uncovered the corruption. She learned a great deal about the dubious if celebrated Eugenie. When Robert had met with her, both he and she had been travelling in Scotland. It was at some ball or other in a Highland castle. "Her hair," they told her, those who began to speak, and perhaps instinctively enlisting the painter in her, "was like full moonglow on ice. Her skin so white it seemed something *made*, not humanly grown – yet vibrant with youth." Eugenie had been nineteen to

Robert's seventeen, but simply to look at them, she appeared the younger. It was high summer then. Deer gleamed through the ripened forests and the mountains caught the sinking sun like shields of porcelain. "They seemed in love," several related. "But already bad things were said about *her*. Yet again, how not? She was – is – very rich – richer even than Robert – and of some ancient family in that peculiar city she comes from. And she looked just a lovely young girl. Although sometimes," some added, lowering their eyes as if ashamed, "a little sulky. Or you heard of nasty little cruelties – some maid's hand she deliberately burned with the hair tongs – or another young woman, of good class, that Eugenie got drunk by some subterfuge, until the victim vomited before the guests, and was disgraced–"

"And," they said, "men died, and even some women. Because Eugenie led them on and then abandoned them. As if they couldn't bear it. As if, thrust off from her, she tore them, and left them with the bleeding wound in their hearts that – slowly, or very fast – drained out their quickness. Nineteen deaths are laid, indirectly, but explicitly, at the door of Eugenie Valotif."

Nineteen deaths. One for each of her years. Twenty now. Like the evening of the letter, the twentieth of December.

"She has no soul," someone observed to Alice, one London afternoon. This was an elderly woman whose niece had been with Eugenie close friends for two months, until Eugenie dismissed her, in an unspecified, unspeakable way, and the niece that night took laudanum and died. "She is a devil."

"*Not* human, then," Alice had murmured.

"Oh, human enough. *Mortal* enough."

And across the delicate array of bone china tea things, Alice's eyes and the old woman's met, for one moment, in a terrible, if speechless and unidentified conclusion. With which the mystical bones of the china concurred.

It was in March, after Alice had learned the exact whereabouts of the Valotif town house in the foreign City, that she heard the legend of St. Yseu.

By then she was quite ready to leave England. Her course was set, her bags were packed.

No one knew her proper reason for visiting France. Just as, outside the intimate circle, few if any knew that Robert Pen-Devon and she had been brother and sister: for reasons of independence, Alice had altered her name the instant she embarked on her career.

Therefore she talked quite freely at the small gallery reception to which her agents had persuaded her, of the journey and its destination. She was travelling there, it went without saying, to paint the historic architectures, the curious slanted up and downhill views, the Roman ruins and the uncanny, corpse-inducing river.

"Ah," said a man, "I too have been to Marcheval."

"What do you think?" asked one of the agents. "Is it worth her going?"

"Oh, more than worth. A glamorous and repulsive place. By turns lovely and disgusting. And full of the most extreme and extraordinary superstitions and biases. They even call the river *Lethe* – or *Styx* – God knows what its real name ever was. Of course that is not uncommon with certain cities. But in Marcheval there are more phantoms to the square yard than in any other spot on earth – even their public houses are named for them. And by the general account almost every street, every alley, bridge or plaza reeks of a past unthinkable horror. I tell you what. They say there's a guided tour of the thoroughfares by night, you know the normal type of thing, where they tell you what vicious killing happened in which lane or house, or where particular haunts and vampires may be regularly come on. Well, it seems this jaunt guarantees to inform and display only the *wholesome* areas, where *no* nauseating atrocity ever took place. It lasts, this walk, all of ten minutes.

The gathering was amused. Alice politely smiled.

One of the women then said, "I remember reading the story of a little saint of Marcheval, St Yseu. The legend is both revolting and – beautiful."

The loud man who had vaunted the City's vileness did not want to be upstaged. But after a while Alice fell into conversation with the woman, and asked what the legend entailed.

"She was the sister of a great sculptor of Mediaeval times, Pierre de Pays. Perhaps you've heard of him? He was known for his alarming images of the Apocalypse and the Judgement of Sheep and Goats. This girl was married and widowed young, after which she became a great benefactress of the poor, fearlessly going among them even in times of plague, to nurse, or to comfort the dying. Then came news that a fleet of ships, lying at anchor in the estuary, found their crews also plague-stricken.

"No one, not even the City priests, would go out to them, but Yseu said that she would, and the brave Pierre rowed her there in a little fishing boat. They did great good, he and she, but when the worst was past, and they were returning to the shore, a huge and monstrous fish suddenly stood up from the sea, towering over the little boat and lunging at Pierre, who had only a knife to defend himself. At this Yseu ran between man and monster. They say she cried out: 'He must live! It is me you shall have.' And sprang into the creature's jaws. It snapped her up, and what it failed to consume was scattered on the water, including her pretty white hands, each bitten off at the wrist. But the fish sank down and was never seen again. And Pierre de Pays lived and went on with his work. And Yseu, of course, was made into saint.

"How pale you've gone, dear Miss Pender. I never meant to distress you. No doubt it's all a lie, of course it is, a silly nonsense."

Alice steadied herself, and agreed the story was silly.

But driving back across the rainy London dark, her thoughts stayed on an image of the sacrificial saint. Such things saints could do. But Robert was already dead, and Alice no saint of any sort.

On that night, in England still, Marcheval reached over sea and land, through geographies and centuries, and touched her with one slender pulse, leaving behind a dainty painless scratch, like the mark of a claw, yet invisible.

Alice dreamed of the river. The river nicknamed forgetfulness.

In the dream it moved so slowly, yet without cease. A twilight crocodile, imperturbably restless: the waters of forgetful night. Which themselves forgot *nothing*. Not a whisper, not a cry. Not a moment. Not a single death.

In the dream, she bent to the river, and drew up, in a clay pot she carried, the river's silver-gray blood, and took it away up a hill, by a wild park where ruins stood from the grass. Farther on, a huge gray face watched her, too, out of the dusk. But Alice did not mind. She had the water now.

Three

"But Mademoiselle Ponday–" this was always how her name was pronounced in the City "–what a novel thing to want to do."

"Not at all," said Alice, in her faultless, if slightly too clever French. "I've heard your river is uncanny. See, already I've gathered some of its water in this little bottle, to study. Don't you think it has a singular shine to it? Yes, your river has unusual properties."

"What can they be? It glitters in sun or freezes in winter and goes dark at night or glows in moonlight; it runs seawards – or backwards to the estuary – as all tidal rivers do; it is full of filth, and stinks. The fish caught there are frisky, but if eaten they poison people. Is not the London river of a similar nature?"

"Quite other," said Alice. "The Thames is a sailor and a story-teller."

The ladies who had called did not take her meaning. The servants kept quiet. Mademoiselle Ponday, being an artist, (not to mention English), must also be eccentric. At least the coachman and the gardener's boy were going down with her this time to the strand, and would help carry back the water.

The afternoon was gusty and huge tectonic clouds bunched over the skyscape. The river had drawn off, leaving the stones and pebbles on its margins. Alice too collected the river water, though none of it in the bottle, let alone the clay vessel of her dream. A few dark boats sloped by. A ragged man, who talked unkindly of and to himself, hunched past, ignoring the water-carriers as they toiled back up the steps to the embankment. The coachman frowned, but the boy seemed cheered by their peculiar little outing. She rewarded both of them, of course, with a generous tip.

The rented house had come with rented servants. Aware what other tenants had been like, on the whole they were tolerant of Alice. Even the coachman forgave her, she saw when, having left the filled metal jars in her studio-room, he quietly advised: "Never put a drop to your lips, mademoiselle."

"It's for use with my painting," she reminded him.

At which he shook his head and out of him sprang a sudden "Be wary of it anyway. As of *her*."

Alice raised her eyebrows. "Who?"

"She. M'mselle Valotif. Never cross her. Never annoy her. Never – in God's good name – never give her your trust or love."

She smiled, and patted his arm, but at the same time said, as she must, "I shall remember what you say, but also, you didn't say one word of it."

"No, m'mselle."

Eugenie had sat for Alice by then for between one and three hours on each of eight consecutive days, during which Alice had sketched her. While Alice did so, the block of paper, board and easel stayed turned away from the subject. The minute one sketch was done, Alice either placed it in a box, the lid of which she then shut and locked – or else she tore the paper methodically into miniscule pieces and tossed them in the studio fire. At no point did Eugenie either protest or move forward with an appeal or demand to see what had been achieved. Neither woman had commented again on the terms of their 'agreement', if so it might be named.

Alice had decided that her subject did as requested from a vague notion Alice wished otherwise, *wanting* to be begged for a preview. Eugenie accordingly would not accommodate her. Or else Eugenie's knack for curiosity was, as a rule, suspended. Having always gained what she desired, she had no need to run ahead of anything. While, like many greedy people, her appetite was also enticed and enhanced by delay. One had heard as much by now of her dealings with many of her lovers. Those who had initially resisted she had treated with the insidious patience of a spider. Her diamante web would enmesh them in the end. And observing the efforts at avoidance no doubt entertained. Alice had not really had to elicit such information through cunning. Gossip in the City was always readily available. But, too, such gossip seemed to seek Alice out on purpose. Even standing in a baker's one early morning, (she often liked to shop for herself), another fragment had fluttered by in her hearing. "They call her sometimes the Viper."

"That poor child, not nine years old, and the bitch sets the dog on him."

"*She* should have to plead for her bread."

"Ah, God *sees*. God only waits."

"He waits too long, and the Devil looks after his own."

But what did Alice and Eugenie talk of, during the sketching sessions? Alice, mostly, of nothing. She uttered only a word or two. And Eugenie herself would sit in silence, only once or twice giving a sort of dulcet command: "I should like tea, now." Or, "Tell them to bring me a glass of wine, would you?" Or, if the sitting had for her gone on too long, "Well, I shall leave you."

Alice never remonstrated. She was the lady's delighted slave. Eugenie was allowing her the greatest joy on earth, for which others struggled, and lacking which they so frequently died,

What power resided in Eugenie, other than that of destruction? Her looks and wealth were mighty – but surely others had had those, if not her ghastly ability, like plague, to level any and all.

Was she a sorceress?

Perhaps, of a kind.

But Alice too knew sorcery, if a different one. And it appeared greedy, incurious, sullen, patient, spiteful, *evil* Eugenie had guessed as much.

The morning following the lugging of Lethe water into the studio, Eugenie arrived as usual, in her dove-gray dress, and arranged herself on the velvet couch.

"Today I begin to paint you, mademoiselle."

"Oh good. I can't stay long." This seemed deliberate, for in most cases the advent of the paint, especially the sensitive medium of a watercolourist, might want more leisure and study even than before.

Alice merely nodded. "Ten minutes will suffice."

And for one heartbeat a crease of disappointment dawned on the sublime face. Then, the lacy little laugh. "My God, how blasé."

"Not at all, mademoiselle. from my sketches I have built and fixed the framework. Now I need only bring the whole to life."

Eugenie, who had seldom said much, now spoke on. "So you are the god, breathing vitality into the inanimate model. It recalls some trashy novel to me – a ridiculous thing – a cadaver raised by lightning–"

"Madame Shelley's *Frankenstein*, perhaps? If not quite."

"Oh, some such dross."

Alice made no reply. She had dipped a brush into a jar of water that, the window lights catching on its glass, seemed to hold an eye of iron fire.

"But there's another tale I heard, an event supposed to have happened in your London – wait–" as if Alice pressed eagerly for knowledge "–a young man whose portrait, a lasting work in oils, took on his old age – while he himself remained young and handsome. Until the picture was destroyed in some way, at which age and defilement fell back on its human subject. Such an absurd tale. Who could make up such idiocy?"

Alice said, "Mr Oscar Wilde. A very great genius."

"English, I suppose."

"Irish, I believe." The brush dipped again, leaving a trail of brilliant nacre in the platinum water, so that briefly the burning iron eye went out. But then came on again. "There now," said Alice. "If you wish, you may go at once." Eugenie stared. "There will be no need for another sitting until – say – the end of the week. Perhaps for twenty minutes, on that occasion."

The guest rose slowly.

"I can't credit this. How on earth can you do justice to the work if–?"

"Quite easily. As I explained. Besides, you've said, you are in a hurry."

Then – only then – Eugenie made a sweeping abrupt advance towards the easel.

Instantly Alice Pender came forward. She stationed herself there, before the reversed and hidden paper, two paintbrushes now in her hand. (Like blades? Surely not.) She looked only quizzical.

"Forgive me, M'mselle Valotif. I would ask you to remember our contract."

"Contract – we have none!"

"Definitely we have. Even though I haven't asked for payment. You must credit this: If you look at the painting before it is complete, I will destroy it. This has happened only once before. I think you will have asked, been told, and may recall the facts of the incident. In our case, I shall lose nothing, since I have charged no fee. Although the thrill and gratification of reproducing your image is recompense enough, one which it would grieve me very much to forego."

It was Eugenie who stood at bay.

But then the awful crystalline spidery complacence reformed to cover her. She turned aside. Disdain traced her face, like a ripple.

"Very well. What a tyrant you are. I shall wait. Do I think it will be worth my while, I wonder?"

"Why else," said Alice, "have you ever set foot here?"

Factually it was untrue that Alice Pender had ever forbidden any of her previous sitters to glimpse a work in progress. Originally, only two clients had ever preferred not to. Both had been old; one a woman and one a man. The woman, whose family had persuaded her to the portrait, openly professed herself nervous at "perceiving what a fine artist will make of my decrepitude." Perhaps Alice's own small legend had grown from these two ventures, the belief that never did she allow anyone who sat for her to regard the work until its completion. In the past three years certainly most of her clients had announced something on the lines of "I know your law. I mustn't look till you have finished me." Alice assured them, flatteringly, that in *their* case it would be no problem if her law was broken. Not all, even then,

Tanith Lee

availed themselves of the chance. That she had ever
destroyed a painting because the invented law was
transgressed was also, patently, false. But this too had
added itself to the myth, and no doubt Eugenie had been
informed of it.

How smug she had looked, even in her little fit of
temper. And how contemptuous. And how *contemptible*.

Was *this* the face that had launched so many
shipwrecks? What had Robert, beautiful and wise and
tender Robert, seen in it to make him cast himself upon
her icy cliff?

Surreptitiously, on the first evening that Alice had met
Eugenie, Alice had watched this creature from a distance,
as it moved about. To Alice, despite the judicious
compliments she soon spread, Eugenie was not beautiful
at all. Yet with all the rest you saw, very definitely, how
men and women both reacted. Though all in differing
forms, plainly they were ravished. Even the ones who,
behind her slender serpentine back, spoke ill of her, were
ravished as well. Their ravishment tinged the very gossip
and the warnings... "Never cross – never annoy – never
give your love!" *But I am not ravished. And so I will not.*

Four

The venue where the painting was first to be shown was the Clock House Gallery. A stoical uphill building, partly dating back to the seventeen hundreds, its Graeco-Roman portico was slicked that evening by the versatile flying sleet of spring.

A note had reached the house with black shutters, at noon. Alice Pender begged her sitter's pardon that she had forgotten to inform Mademoiselle Valotif that, rather than – as intended – awarding her a private showing beforehand, Miss Pender had been forced to display the finished portrait to the general public that very night, and for a week after, due to a prior arrangement made by her agents with the gallery management . Miss Pender deeply regretted any annoyance this might cause. She trusted Mademoiselle Valotif would see her way to forgiving the blunder. Maybe, Alice suggested, Eugenie could simply visit the gallery, not mentioning to anyone that it was her own portrait on view. Along with any of the public then present, she might look at it, even in a certain privacy. For it was a strange fact, others did not always recognise the subject of a painting as *being* the subject. Occasionally even the subject themselves might be surprised.

Along with every particle Eugenie had learned of Alice's skill and repute, Eugenie had doubtless heard that Miss Pender's sitters were always astonished, and never dissatisfied. While even general viewers marvelled, both at the utter verisimilitude of the likeness, and some extraordinary vista of each person's *inner* self, captured by the image. The old lady, for example, who had been afraid to see her physical decline, saw indeed an old woman portrayed, but one whose age had added a profound potency to a form still possessed of prettiness and flare. While the fat and clumsy grocer, in secret a generous benefactor and loyal friend, showed in his portrait a radiance that gave the faithfully rendered coarseness of his face the theatrical dignity of a great king, when acted by an actor of magnitude.

What happened then when Eugenie received the apologetic note? Did fury bound through her? If so, was it very quick? It came, it went – and how did it leave her in its wake, narrow-eyed and white? Did her thoughts run in any predictable mode, as: Oh, she knew at once this was Alice's trick? The mercantile agility of Alice, evidently, had made up its mind that, unpaid by Eugenie, still the artist must grab money from the job. And thus she sold Eugenie Valotif – *she*, even *she* – to the highest bidder. Even if the portrait would be common property only one week, and then most carefully removed to the Valotif house, the insult had been delivered.

Or did her thoughts run on those plans Eugenie herself had had, (had she?), perhaps of throwing a party and showing off the portrait there privately, to a rush and hush of the chosen and enthralled? And must *she* go then, like every ordinary gawper, and gawp communally in the gallery? *No*, she would not do it. *No*.

Whatever she thought, she penned in turn a note to Alice. The words of it had a spiky shape, thorns of black ink incised on and in creamy paper.

The note concerned the English habits of incompetence and rudeness, always linked, not to forget the constipated financial priorities of a nation of petty shopkeepers. And off went the note into the afternoon.

But no reply came back from the rented house close to the Academy.

Then she *must* go, Eugenie, must she not? Anyone – even an Eugenie – must. To confront Alice Pender at the gallery if nothing else. Not a word need be spoken. A glance, a look, would be enough. And this picture. This painting. This watercolour. This portrait. This reproduction of *herself* .

What would that be, then?

Dressed like a shining star, all diamonds, out of her house Eugenie stepped. Into her carriage. Along the streets, up the hills. Darkness was smoking like a vast wet bonfire in the sky. The electric lamps of the gallery glared fearlessly before them, too ignorant to be scared.

What is said now?

"Ah, Mademoiselle Valotif, you are most welcome. M'mselle Pender assured us you would honour us with your attention tonight. Please – up the Long Stair to the Orchid Annexe. There is champagne from the south. And here a white rose, pray take it, mademoiselle. So glorious to receive you here, on such an evening, when we are able to display the latest work by such a talent as M'mselle Pender..."

And Eugenie, did she ask if M'mselle Pender had yet arrived?

If she did, then or presently: "Alas, she has been called away. To England. She must catch the overnight packet, it seems – some emergency of a family nature–"

Did the diamonds trickle dull a moment, or flash like kicked coals?

Up the Long Stair however, up into the Orchid Annexe with its petalled walls, and a number of little paintings and sketches, (examples of works by Alice

Pender), where people paused, lingered, or only stood chattering to each other of different matters which, perhaps, the artwork had called into their brains. A liveried person came and Eugenie accepted, as all of them had done, a glacial shallow bowl, modelled in popular fancy from the breast of a dead queen. Diamond spangle next of champagne bubbles.

At the long room's long end, something upright on an easel of jet black wood, and with two long marble-white curtains closed across.

If Eugenie had stopped, frozen or incandescent, acquaintances must have drifted to her.

"It's quite a joke, isn't it – no one knows whom this portrait represents. And the Pender girl isn't here – her brother is ill, or something, in London – But surely, M'mselle Valotif – she was to have painted *you*, was she not?"

And if that was said, what then did Eugenie reply? Was it in the affirmative, the negative, a mere evasion, a *delay* – conceivably all of these. Or none. Only a look of incomprehension, or secret knowledge. Possibly she answered, "Oh, M'mselle Pender has told *me* who has been painted here. But I was sworn to silence. An oath it would be crass to betray."

White curtains shut the picture and hide it. Why not go and tear them apart?

Black night shuts the windows, and night *cannot* be torn undone. Nor anything, everything night hides, be laid bare, which may include immortality or everlasting death.

At eight o'clock, (imprecisely, going on the multitude of clocks that were thick as the spines on a porcupine in that region), the portrait was unveiled.

By that hour many of the attendees were drunk, or at least aglow, from the endless breastfuls of excellent champagne.

Eugenie was not drunk. Could it be probable she was capable of it?

The manager of the gallery, in his black and white, gave a short speech, confirming that the picture was untitled, and regretting the sad absence of the artist herself, which he too attributed to the severe illness of a sibling.

Then two assistants came forward, and with a measured gesture, faultless, parted the curtains as one.

And there, attached safely to its board and so to the easel, unframed and with no glass before it, revealed in the fearless glare of the electricity, it was. The watercolour portrait.

A gush of sound resulted, not much of words expressed, more breaths drawn in. Then a soft scatter of giggles as at some insalubrious jest. And then, the exclamations.

"Who *is* it?"

"Whoever can it *be*?"

"Why *this* portrait? Could she find nobody else?"

"Her work usually has–"

"Such finesse. I've never seen a Pender, and credit me, I've followed her opus more than somewhat, that wasn't at the very least... what can I say?"

"Is this intellectually *valid*?"

"It will either raise her reputation to the height of the gods – or ruin the woman."

"Ruin her without doubt."

"But the painting – the brushwork – is itself technically superb! Look at the care with which–"

"Yes, a travesty."

Eugenie swallowed the last of her champagne. She turned to leave the Annexe. At the head of the stairs outside, the gallery manager himself hastened towards her. "Mademoiselle, please wait one moment. I must thank you most heartily. Your generosity in allowing the work to be exhibited before your own claim is realised – forgive me, but of course I am aware it was you yourself who commissioned the work. Let me assure you, we will transport it to your home in seven days, with the utmost attention. Such a clever work, a work of genius and courage. And, dear Mademoiselle, naturally I have observed to the letter your wish to remain anonymous. M'mselle Pender was absolute in her instructions. No one knows it is your property. Like the subject, the owner remains, and ever will remain unknown." Eugenie must have stood there, her face fixed in its normal placid avidity, or if at all altered, unnoticeably to this jolly gentleman. Who added at the last, unable to resist, it seemed, "She is, perhaps, the lady in the painting, some relative? It strikes me, pardon me if I presume, that I can detect just the *faintest* resemblance – a wisp, a nuance – before of course she–"

But down the Long Stair the woman owner of the unidentified portrait was already travelling. Like a cluster of firework stars she passed away through the hall, and out into the undrawn black of light-lit Marcheval.

Five

Painted mostly in tones of gray, from the darkest to the palest shades, and where not in gray in metallic tones, like iron and silver, or mercury, or an unearthly electric sort of phosphorescence, or like stones, even flesh-coloured stones, but the flesh transparently gray, as though under the weight of a depthless winter river. It was a masterpiece, the picture. Yet so in advance of its time and situation, few would see as such. Besides the subject was not, then, generally to anybody's taste.

She – a female – seemed to be about sixty years old. But it was difficult to be quite sure of her age. She was not exactly fat, but vastly bloated, in a type of fish-like manner, if without the flexibility and grace of a fish. She looked somewhat, (as one critic declared, who had attended the gallery showing), as if she had been coerced into drinking gallons of water, as some lunatics did, or beer, as drunkards of the 'lower orders' did. Until she had swollen up nearly to bursting. You wanted, disgustingly, he added, to "stick a pin in her and exfluidate her distended bulk", which was like that of a dead pike or carp, and so "relieve her of all that *pressure.*"

Her hair was gray, of a very faded tint, and thin, so that despite its ferocious updressing, and the mother-of-pearl combs that held it, gaps were visible of a pallidly inflamed scalp. Some ulcers too were to be seen on her neck. Not richly coloured, these also were gray, like diseased fish-scales, or something from a dead lizard.

She had lizard's eyes. They were *no* colour, not even gray. Nothing looked out of them. That was, an awful and very animate negative awareness, which represented what Nothing must be – an absence that *is* a presence, a void, an abyss always hungry – that *Nothing* it was, which looked out and straight into the eyes of the petrified viewer. No one, even the ones who then, and later, admired this disconcerting work, could meet the gaze of the painted woman for even a minute. About seven to twelve seconds was the most one could bear.

The woman's face had fallen, kept together only by its swelling. The ulcerated bulbous neck likewise. The hands were like veined bags, with bag-fingers, having chalky nails. Her gown was prosperous – but gray, and it was a silk sack. The chair she sat in was hard to see, though it looked black, like the easel, or a tree in winter. But she filled it up, and even the *chair* gave an impression that it was being destroyed by the woman's presence in it. Behind her, shadows – gray, metallic, electric, watery – hung as if in escort. She was lit by no light. Yet she shone as a corpse might if left for long enough.

The gallery manager who had spoken of a relative had been attempting to please Eugenie Valotif. To console her. He had uneasily concluded Eugenie must lovingly value this hash of human detritus, (who certainly was dying of an incurable sickness, *or* else driven to some obscene depravity by sorrows impossible to imagine, let alone to bear). Love was blind, one knew. And Eugenie's love for the diseased old hag had prompted the commissioning – even the *showing* – of the portrait. Therefore to praise it, and suggest a noted likeness just visible through the layers of degeneration, were not beyond his scope. That same night, lying down with one of his young friends, the poor man had begun to weep. "I'm so sorry for the dear little Valotif girl. What an appalling thing. It must be some aunt, or grandmother...

and still to see loveliness and *lovingness* in such a putrescent, sodden monstrosity."

"Well, but Charles," playfully quipped his young lover, "I find you delicious, and look at the mess you are."

So nights and hearts might be saved, or lost.

Her portrait, (nameless), was brought to the door of its (nameless) owner on the prescribed day, about ten in the morning.

It was masked once more, now in linen and wool and protective boards. Up the stairs of the house with black shutters it was borne. And into a narrow room, barely the width of a big sofa, and with a window like a thin finger, looking on stripped trees and massed roofs that gathered below, in a rebellious if noiseless and motionless horde.

A temporary position, no doubt.

In a while the painting would be framed and hung where it could be seen and appreciated. Assuming one had, it went without saying, a strong stomach.

But the mistress of the house was from home that day. She had had to go to the country.

A servant, extensively, frightenedly careful of Eugenie's orders, saw the hidden object in, then – the men dismissed – locked the door of the narrow room, returning the key to a desk on the upper storey.

"Heaven knows what it is. Some precious artwork, I suppose. Christ help us all if it isn't right for her."

Spring *became* spring, and next summer strode through Marcheval, swishing its tail and lifting its maned head to roar.

And then the fall of autumn. And after that, once

more, the winter twilight of frost and snow.

Over and again this happened, these bizarre metamorphoses defined as seasons. No one questioned them. What would be the use?

A space of three years went by in their clutches, and another new spring began.

The house near the Academy was being rented by a foul-tempered historian, busy with researching the annals of the City, and quite prone to inebriated vandalism. The rented servants put up with him perforce, and wished him anathema behind his back.

The other, cream-stuccoed house, with black shutters, had stood empty for countless months. It had passed, in some legacy of an automatic nature, (the owner left no will), but the lucky recipient so far did not take up residence. Now and then a caretaker visited the property, prowled it for an hour, and came away louring. Rats in the walls, he said. Birds in the attics. Rot and damp from proximity to the river. A bad smell in several rooms. Bricks out elsewhere. He reported to associates on the *feel* of the place, which was not to be endured. It was haunted, or cursed. God knew what had gone on there. Some rich and feted young woman had lived in it, had she not? Then gone away – that could hardly account for anything. "Whenever I must go in there," the caretaker appended, "I wear my cross – the blessed cross from the little chapel by Our Lady of Lights. Without that, I swear I'd never get over the threshold."

He seldom, either, with or without his cross, ventured upstairs. The upper apartments, a set of lady's rooms especially, were some of the worst. Both for decay and depression. There was a locked room, too. It seemed very narrow and small, and if outside you looked up, it had a grubby blind drawn down over the tiny window. Some closet then, even a lavatory. He was never tempted to gain an entry.

When or if the new owner eventually stirred himself to take possession, gangs of workmen and cleaners would be needed, flooding the premises with coarse and resuscitating life. But no one knew when that would be. Until then, leave well alone. Or leave ill alone. That was wise enough.

Epilogue

"What a beautiful young man!" the visitor exclaimed, as he entered the drawing room.

"Yes. He was my brother. Robert Pen—Devon."

"But this is a recent portrait?"

"Last Christmas. I painted it then, but from memory. Somehow I never thought to paint him while he lived. Perhaps I didn't need a picture then."

Tirso turned and stared at her, if rather meekly. "I believe I heard something of Sir Robert's death – a tragic accident on his estate–"

Alice noted her visitor seemed less brutal than inquisitive; not cruel – *feral* was the best word.

"He hanged himself, monsieur. He was seventeen."

"My God. Oh, you must excuse me, Miss Pender. But the painting is quite wonderful, most arresting. Please forgive me if I say that, at least in this way, you have given him immortality."

Alice smiled graciously. "Won't you sit down? There, perhaps, by the fire. And we must have tea, perhaps some brandy. I'm afraid our English springs are often malicious. *Ah!* Then you've heard my nickname, monsieur, I see."

Tirso had lowered his eyes in a pretence of naive shyness, like a sleek cat just caught with a paw on the canary's cage.

"Yes," Alice continued. "I do know about it. M'Alice Pender. But your name is Spanish, I think."

Tirso had sat down. "My mother," he said, lightly offering Alice his illegitimacy as a sop. "But I live mostly in France. And for the past six years in Marcheval City where you yourself have sojourned, though briefly."

"A few weeks."

"I hope they were rewarding ones."

"Oh yes," said Alice Pender.

She must be now almost thirty years of age. Physically, Tirso thought, she looked much less, but there was to her demeanour, her contained and collected serenity, watchful yet self-assured, the method of a woman far older.

The tea arrived, in attractive rather than fine china, a decanter or two, and a tray of *petits fours* much in the French style.

Her cool, thoughtful hospitality matched with everything he had gleaned about her, She was comfortably well off, without being rich, and lived her independent life lacking either scandal or mediocrity. There had been one or two lovers, of course, but these affairs were so discreet no opprobrium attached itself. Tirso, whose carnal tastes were for the male sex, appreciated the expertise with which Alice had organized her own.

He liked her talent too. He liked all those paintings of hers he had seen, many of them portraits, very greatly. All but one. And nobody, as far as he knew, (he knew by now quite a lot), even where rating highly the mastery of the piece, actually *liked* that one – and recently many journals had carried its photograph, and critics written of it. In common artistic parlance it was currently titled the *Portrait in Gray*. It had even, here and there, become useful as an expression. For example: "I'd prefer to spend an evening locked in a room with the *Portrait in Gray* – than another five minutes with so and so." Or: "Vile-looking? It was nearly worse than the *Portrait in Gray*."

Alice had never explained or excused the work. Nor had she ever given away the name of the patron for whom she had painted it, let alone that of the actual sitter.

Only poor Charles had partially done that, and only once. To Tirso, then his lover, that night after the picture's debut at the gallery on Clock House Hill.

Inquisitive and feral – as a *lynx* – though Tirso was, he did not incriminate his friends. He had promised the tearful Charles he would never speak of the revelation that glued the Gray Portrait to Eugenie Valotif. Nor had he. But he had been instantly intrigued. A young man of independent means, his main creative outlet had become the study of his fellow humans. Even when obsessively enamoured of them, he would study them. Which practice had sometimes annulled the liaison.

To begin with he began to attend the Orchid Annexe of the gallery for about an hour every day. At that time he was doubtless the only one to loiter by the Gray Portrait. Others came – and went, nearly always with smothered expressions of distaste. (One young woman swooned and had to be supported from the vicinity). On a single visit, a man angrily asked Tirso outright why he stood by the nightmarish painting so long. "I don't look in its eyes," Tirso had mystically replied, "that's the secret."

The thing was however that, during the week when he studied it, before its delivery to the Valotif house, Tirso started to notice a fearful, unbelievable clue. Despite letting slip the connection to the picture's patron, Charles had not relayed to Tirso any slight similarity discovered between Mademoiselle Valotif and the repulsive bladder in the painting. Whether Charles had really perceived such an element was anyway cause for debate. If he had, it must have been by a sort of skewed luck. Tirso though, staring and patrolling and staring again, *did* begin to see the resemblance. For incredibly it was there. Nor did Tirso, for the blink of an eye, suppose it any familial likeness he had uncovered. *Oh* no. One lynx may always detect the darling, dangerous patterns of a fellow lynx. It seemed Alice – M'alice – Pender was, in her own fashion, another of Tirso's kind. Alice was a lynx, and she had unsheathed her claws. No wonder la Valotif had, at the picture's unmasking, fled the scene. Tirso had watched her do it.

But what had Eugenie done so to enrage Alice? Something epic it must be. For Alice had painted Eugenie, by anyone's standard a superlatively beauteous specimen, as the malformation on the paper. Maybe representing Eugenie, when old and in the last stages of some terminating illness. What she would come to look like, then? Yet too with all the hallmarks on her swollen face and body of a lifetime of subhuman viciousness. One glance at that face showed it naked. A dying devil was there, but one *damned, poisoned* by its own self.

Tirso made it his quest to search out and oversee the Valotif house. He began to idle regularly in a public garden close by. Meanwhile, he learned all he could from gossip, from newspapers, from any available source, all he might concerning Eugenie. And the same for Alice Pender.

This accumulation built itself, bit by bit, into a pair of towering ziggurats. But Alice's was rather wonderful, and gemmed in and out by quiet genius. Eugenie's was an inverted cesspit, decorated with slabs of rotting meat and the broken bones of souls.

Two days after the show at the gallery, Eugenie

emerged from her house. Tirso beheld her step into her carriage.

He saw too her beauty seemed a little different. He could not get his mind to analyse it quite, what the change was. His mind... seemed reluctant to complete the task.

Over the next few days Tirso watched Eugenie go in or come out again, with at last a mass of baggage dragged before her. Into the carriage the baggage went, and so did she. From this excursion she did not immediately return.

And during her absence the portrait was brought from the gallery, and carried in, like a coffin, with a backward motion.

Seven further days. During which the frigid spring abruptly advanced, violently pulling open buds and throwing showers of sparrows in the air. Flowers and other entrants scattered the park. Tirso crossed to the house with black shutters and knocked on the door. It seemed Mademoiselle had gone to the country. She might be away a further week.

Tirso then became involved, as he had not meant to be, in a new exciting love-affair. Life will always interrupt anything, or death. No one yet has been able to teach either of them good manners.

It was early summer when Tirso, himself in a carriage driving up towards the Temple-Church, spotted a woman, in an elaborate white costume, on the street. His first thought had been she was really too full in the figure for such a pure and glistening white. And her hair seemed to need washing –

Then, as they trotted by, he saw her face. It was Eugenie. She was standing outside one of the fashionable if quaint little shops that had started to litter the area.

And before her lay a parcel she had dropped. She seemed not able to pick it up. And nobody, so far, had sprung to her aid.

Tirso had his friend stop the carriage. Jumping out and hurrying back, he scooped the parcel from the ground and held it out to her.

She looked at him, not attempting to accept it. It was as if she had to recall where she was, and who. Her face appeared less pale than pasty, like dough which had begun to sour. Her eyes seemed filmed. And then, like an unnerving electric light switched suddenly on, the leer of an aging coquette suffused her countenance. It was too brilliant a light, too descriptive. Her teeth were sallow. A stale odour hung about her.

"Oh, thank you, monsieur."

The parcel was taken. "My pleasure, madame." Thank God his friend just then called peevishly from the cab.

"Forgive me," blurted Tirso, lynx eyes shining like knife-edges. He sprinted from her presence, and kept his own council, although the friend asked him, "Who is that ugly old slut?"

"I have no notion. I acted gallantly to impress you."

But now Tirso's mind had caught up with its task. It leapt about in the confines of his skull. He felt a glorious terror and a shrinking, disgraceful joy. He had encountered witchcraft.

Not until that autumn did Eugenie Valotif retreat permanently to her second house, in the hills north and west of Marcheval.

Pine trees studded this portion of the upland, hammered into the earth like spiked black nails, their heads flattened by two or three centuries of winter winds.

Even fifteen years before there had been stories of wolves. But it was now doubtful.

Tirso knew nothing of them.

What he knew was this:

All the servants had either been dismissed from the town house, or else had left, in a sort of tidal wave. Rather, as one of Tirso's trusted gossips informed him, like the sinking ship abandoning its single giant rat. (The rat presumably being Eugenie). It seemed her always execrable behaviour and spite had escalated over recent months. She had become fat and out of sorts, her hair even succumbing to some type of malady and falling out. A dressmaker, who had diligently returned with a gown measured up only a day previously, had been concussed by the scent flagon Eugenie flung at her head, on finding the gown already too tight by several inches. Tired of her hurlings and scaldings, her vituperative outbursts – both coarse and blasphemous – the servants took themselves off. By then it was reckoned a large number of respectable people guessed that no servant worth their salt would remain in her employ. To have left la Valotif had become a recommending reference in itself.

But some servants, they said, stayed in the northern country house. One dusk Eugenie, who latterly never went out by day, set off for the hills.

Tirso's love-affair had just been dismantled. He had nothing much to do, and so resumed an interest in the subject of Alice Pender's revenge. He learned of Eugenie's retreat inside the month.

He himself packed a bag, and left the City by train.

A prosperous village lay not three miles from the Valotif country house. He put up at an inn, which endeared itself to him by being, (he thought), exactly like a hostelry from the seventeenth century.

The following morning he walked to the gates of the country house.

It was a soft autumn, only sprinkled with stops and starts of forgetful rain. But the neglected drive was puddled, and the building itself showed no signs of occupation.

An aproned servant nonetheless opened the door.

Indeed, m'mselle was at home. But she did not ever rise yet.

Tirso generously reassured the woman he would wait, and was conducted, with a sturdy indifference he liked, to a chilly gloomy salon on the second floor.

Here he found a piano, untuned inevitably, but raising the cranky lid he sat down on the stool, and commenced to crash out merry mazurkas and threatening impromptus. He was reasonably proficient, and certainly loud. The house rang at the cacophony. Its deserted beehive of chambers, most either lacking furniture or else with it turned to phantoms by dust-sheets, gave back the notes of the music like a jamboree.

The clock had given up its ghost, but his own watch told him it was after three when the servant reappeared in the doorway.

"Thee may go up," said she.

And up he went.

He was thrilled to find himself by now frightened. He was on edge merely thinking he would *see* Eugenie, and alarmed as well she might remember their brief encounter over the parcel.

He was wondering too if she had brought with her here, the picture, even if still in its wrappings.

As he climbed the third tall flight of stairs, stone steps,

for the house was quite old, Tirso rehearsed the interview he had formerly had with a little lady's maid in the City, at the flat of one of his tame gossips. "Rénee said m'mselle'd go there, to that narrow room where they'd put the picture, and she'd stand outside the door, sometimes for half an hour. They all saw her do it! Even the man that cleaned the windows."

"But did she never go in?"

"Oh no, monsieur, though she always had the key in her hand as if she meant to. So far as anybody knows, that painting's still tied up in its boards."

"And she only stood by the door?"

"Yes, monsieur. Sort of as if she were – *listening*, Rénee says. *Listening*. And her face like a lump of crumpled newspaper. She'd got fat then, and there were blotches and pimples on her skin. What funny things rich people do, don't they, getting themselves painted and then never going to look at it?"

"But you think then the portrait must be of Mademoiselle Valotif?"

"I've never seen it, of course. How could any of us ever have seen – how'd we dare? But stands to reason. Perhaps it was," and the voice dropping low, as the parcel dropped low on to the street, "that she'd got so nasty-looking then, she couldn't bear to see how she'd been, how that artist must have painted her, before, when she was attractive. Oh –! Thank you, monsieur! But that's too much money – well, if you're sure. You're very charitable. My poor mother will be most grateful. And the little ones."

The upper door, when he reached it, was partly ajar. Tirso knocked.

There was no response. Except all at once – a vague

sluggish shuffling noise. It might have been the sound a huge and ancient serpent made, as it hauled itself from one spot to another.

He walked into the room. A big room, with ranks of glass panes, by which eldritch curtains hung, thick brocade grizzled by dust and webs. Outside, the pale gray afternoon, tending towards its end.

Something sat in a satin chair before a central casement. It had turned its head to observe him.

A shudder plunged through Tirso, the length of his body. He had never felt anything like it... except in the throes of passion – although this time it was not pleasant.

The Pender painting was in the satin chair.

But it was *not* the painting. This was entirely of three dimensions, of human dimensions, though distorted. Yet to its portrait it was identical. A facsimile, perfect even to the rubbery context of the swollen skin, the *'fluidation'*, the gross unnatural bulges and thick folds, the lesions of the ulcerated flesh, and the hair unthreaded through mother-of-pearl combs, and the colourless leaden eyes – that still held in them – oh yes – the devilish abnormality that was dying there, inside a slough of despond solely made from its own corrupt chemistry. A smell lay on all the room. Perhaps throughout the whole house. He had mistaken it, he thought, for the damp and mildew, the stale dirtiness of a neglected building. It carried a faint reek of river water too. A deep river full of rotten things.

He stared, and the creature stared back.

Did it recognise him – did it know him even for a man? Could it even *see*?

And then it spoke.

"Why, monsieur, how determined you are. You have found me out in my sanctuary. Most amusing." The spangled tone of the diamond coquette, coming up from below a mile of polluted river, out of the corpse-mud, out of the lungs of Hell.

"I–" said Tirso. It was all he could achieve.

But "Splendid, the carriage is ready. Shall we go at once?" went on the seated thing, and lumbered and billowed to its feet. It came lurching, rolling towards him. He believed he would lose consciousness, but he was much too acute for that. He pelted to the door and held it very wide.

Out ahead of him poured the abomination, and on to the stairs, and began to descend like – an octopus, perhaps, sliding over undersea rocks, yet not coordinated, not rational.

Tirso stood at the stair-head, and watched. He must hold on to a banister. He was shaking from head to foot. But the grotesque slopped and slithered on, fluttering behind it the train of a vast gray snail-trail of silk robe that, just as in the painting, swathed and hid, thank God, all but its bloated hands, and bloated feet, (in cloth shoes torn open from forcing), and the distended neck, and head under a skimp of ashy cotton hair.

Tirso found he had let go the banister and, with grim nausea and trepidation, he was now creeping down the stairs behind the apparition. As if to escort her – it. As if it – she had him on a strong and unbreakable leash. In that manner they approached the ground floor, and there Tirso, (now navigating the last flight), beheld the indifferent and aproned peasant woman, who seemed the only servant here, walk into the hallway below.

"I am going out," said the voice of the coquette in the river-basement.

"As thee say, m'mselle."

Sturdy cow, *she* did not flinch. She was solid granite.

"With the gentleman," the sewer voice added. "To the City."

The obliging servant gave a crabbed part-curtsy, and undid the two leaves of the door, and there outside were the gardens, and the declining afternoon. And the autumn rain, which was abruptly being emptied out again over the landscape. And a fresh-born and nippy wind.

A gust of combined air and water blew headlong into the hall, as if it had been waiting outside for hours, only longing to gain admittance. On the antique stone floor drops of moisture speckled like sweat.

Tirso could see no carriage ready on the drive. Nor did the servant make any move to summon one.

The obtuse – if it was – uncandour of *her* face gave him, he found, a kind of stupid courage. He did not take another step.

Unlike the fall storm, for a second rush of it dashed through into the hall, this one more energetic and pronounced. (The softest thunder-clap tactfully murmured overhead).

And the creature in gray seemed suddenly to pirouette, spinning right around.

Tirso reached out once more and caught at the stair rail. He thought his eyes were to blame. What was he seeing?

Eugenie Valotif, (if still the thing might be said to be her, as though she herself, now, were only *untitled, unnamed*), had become flat as a playing card. And if she was, she was the Queen of Rains. All her grayness glittered with the splash of tempests, all her bulk, though hugely spread and described, was now *without* dimensions. She was like a colossal square of paper. Or no, she was not the paper, merely she had been drawn upon it, and behind her, rather than the weather-wet and blustery day, odd shadowy and metallic hints and glintings, like webs and traceries and smoke. But even as Tirso peered at this, (his eyes partially closed up, as if in too strong light), he saw how the dash of the rain was dissolving her, all of her bloated gelatinous shape and form, every feature, every blemish and thread of skin or hair. She was *running*, like liquid from a jar. *Spilling* off the paper.

"There now, monsieur's thrown up all over the hall floor, which me, or some other luckless one, must be made to clean. But I'm done with any of that, here, so no matter."

Through his ringing ears Tirso heard the servant's short speech.

He wiped his mouth, and sat down on the third stair, his head hanging.

"You saw it," he said.

She said nothing.

Finally he was able to look up at her.

"You *saw*, madame, what happened."

"Did I?" Her shrewd eyes seemed only sly and angry.

But then she – pretending probably – relented a fraction. "Thee does see things, thee must, if thee lives as long as I. Oh yes, for your sort middle age is nothing. But for mine it's an achievement. I saw a bit of paper blown in, all wet from the rain."

"Then where is your – where is *she*?"

The woman in the apron straightened and folded her arms. "M'mselle does as she desires. And I'm dismissed. What should I care? Were thee one of her lapdogs, too?

Then thee've been spared. She was like the Black Death, her, thee is fortunate to get off."

Tirso laughed. He had not meant to.

At which she did too. He gave her some money, which she took from him with an oath, not at all like the nice little maid in the gossip's flat.

There was nothing on the stone floor, it was dry of anything that had run down there, even of the speckle of rain. And outside by then the storm was ruffling away along the hills towards the City.

One imagined, or miss-saw, all sorts of events. Or told oneself one did.

The servant said then she must shut up the house, or her mistress would be furious, and her mistress could be harsh when annoyed. When crossed. But too, even when trusted and loved, m'selle could be murderous.

He visualised the servant shutting the house, going round locking doors with huge cold keys, all this as he walked back to the inn and the village. Afternoon autumn sun came out during the last quarter mile, and beamingly showed him uncountable types of watery designs on the landscape, streams and pools and puddles and dripping pine trees. Eugenie was in none of them. She had been washed well away, and sucked down by stone into the bowel of the abyss.

Was he ill for a while? No, surely not anything so severe. A touch out of sorts, as sometimes one might be, returning to the City and ordinary pastimes, after a small vacation...

Assailed he was, however, by a constant inner debate: had he truly *seen* what he thought he had? Or was it a delusion, the servant woman an accomplice, maybe, seeming to uphold the first idea that the irrational had happened. And then cementing in the second idea, that this being so, one should ignore it. He had heard of people who could walk safely through perilous slices of the world, by the straightforward expedient of *making out* nothing inimical was near them.

Certainly, when he went back to re-visit his gossips, either they had gone away somewhere or other – like the nice little maid – or there was something much more fascinating on their menu: Somebody stabbed, or some banking conspiracy, such stuff. Eugenie? Oh. She was still at her country place, was she not? Or had she gone East, for better weather?

The house of black shutters, he did discover, stayed empty, with eventually only a careless caretaker. Yet Tirso never now sought the house. He was too indolent. Or prudent.

In lieu of all that then, Tirso commenced a quite serious contemplation of the work of Alice Pender.

He consequentially fell in love with her paintings. Once, he bought one; he was just able to afford it, a framed watercolour sketch not twelve inches by eight, of an English 'Saxon' oak tree, standing alone and regal in a stubbled field.

And time went on going by, the seasons, the sun and moon as ever appearing to push and pull it so it had no choice. Left to itself the poor bloody thing would much rather, no doubt, have paused. "Let me sit down," Time would say, "just for a century. Just here, this enchanting summer sunset. And that way the rest of you can all stay as young as you are for a hundred years." (Tirso, young, forgot others would *not* be young any longer at this point, and must therefore put up with a century of ailing and arthritic old age. Not to consider perhaps, a century of the very instant of *dying*. To his credit, he did think of it three decades after). In any case, time did not sit down and a handful of years did pass. And one night at a dinner he met Charles again.

Something wonderful took place. From lovers they found they were now able simply to be close friends.

In the course of this friendship, it was Tirso Charles meant to enlist, when the subject of the Gray Portrait flew home to roost.

"The new owner, the inheritor, has decided to move into the Valotif town house. It's in a sorry state and will cost thousands to repair. But of course, now, the heir to the Valotif fortune *has* a superfluity to lavish on it. *Well*. It seems they broke into an upper room – the door had warped – there were rats and pigeons everywhere else – and there in a corner was a painting, from which the boards and wrappings had, in the process of desuetude, fallen off."

Tirso had gone pale. Which startled *him*, not Charles – who, in the civilized non-electric lamplight, did not notice.

"It was *the* portrait, Tirso. Do you recall? The untitled work of Mademoiselle Pender, which Mademoiselle Valotif loaned to the gallery all those years ago."

"I... I do recall."

"A masterpiece, I've always said so. And public taste is so much better educated nowadays. But needless to relate, the male Valotif heir let out a shriek and said if *It* stayed on the premises he would have it burned, and the house around it! What melodramatics. Yet it leads the fellow to offer the painting, gratis, to my gallery–" (it was, the gallery on Clock House Hill, the property of

Charles at this era) "–only my trouble is, despite securing the best lawyers, no bill of sale, nor any document, seems to survive to prove the picture ever *belonged* to the Valotifs. Instead, it looks as if it had negligently been left with Mademoiselle Valotif, which knowing her charms is possible. But she is presumed dead, and since the picture's refinding, one must presume too the artist might like it back. Now Tirso," Charles added, refilling their crystal goblets with black champagne, "*you* are the adventurous and intelligent one, the – in the most aesthetic way – *seducer*. Do you think if we funded your journey, you could risk the filthy French Channel, and attempt London, to persuade Mademoiselle – I should say *Miss* Pender – to sell us the work? I can organize a reasonable sum. I sincerely suppose, in twenty odd years, this portrait will be among the most famous and influential of the modern world. It might even rate with Leonardo – if not entirely for beauty or finesse, then for sheer *uniqueness*."

Tirso drank his champagne. He said, "You're certain Eugenie Valotif is thought to be dead?"

"It must be so. She vanished – what was it? – four, five, six years ago. This was at the house in the hills, apparently. The villagers say there mademoiselle went out, was missing, and never returned. The house was all locked up, the furniture in sheets. It showed few signs of having been lived in. The police investigated and got nowhere at all. A universal rumour has it the girl drowned herself for unrequited love in some obscure and unlocated pond. A dreadfully unoriginal fate. And she was exquisite. Probably you never took that in. Divine. Though, I have to say, rather rigid. Rather – shallow."

"And the portrait," said Tirso with a – to Charles

pedantic – insistence, "it really was *found*?"

"I've seen it, my dear. It is the self same article. Just as disturbing and extraordinary. A work of genius, I've no doubt."

"Strange," said Tirso, as if to himself, "somehow I thought it might have... been destroyed. Fallen to bits – or the paint... run."

"Oh, watercolours nowadays are frankly stolid, dearest boy. It takes more than a lick of damp to vanquish them. Well, what do you say? Will you go to London for us, for me, and hypnotise Miss Pender into letting us keep the work?"

"And that, then, is my errand," said Tirso to Alice those months after, seated in her spring drawing room and eating *petits fours*.

"You – the gallery – wish to buy the painting from me?"

"Very much so. Although with the proviso that the price can't be too high." He named an indeed not insulting sum. Then lowered his eyelashes to show what a vulgarity details of cash must be to either of them.

Alice Pender gazed into her fire.

She said, rather as Tirso had said it, "I'd heard they're certain Mademoiselle Valotif had died."

Tirso also gazed into the fire.

For both of them maybe, for a second, the blazing flames turned silver, and through the smart room a hiss of shadows and metals and dire secrets that dripped slime, swam like water from an undead river.

"Perhaps you will need time to consider," Tirso said. "I'm afraid the payment can't be made more sumptuous – taxes, such inanities. But the esteem, I assure you–"

Alice raised her eyes, but not to him. Above the mantelpiece the thrilling other portrait hung, the handsome, almost angel-like young man: Robert Pen-Devon.

"I hope you will allow me to say," said Tirso quietly, "that this picture here, that of your brother, is among the most spiritually engaging I've ever seen. It would bring a blessing on any wall it ornamented. Yet–"

"Yet," said Alice, as softly as he.

"Yet the *Portrait in Gray* is a work of such power and significance, the hand of some god seems to have guided your own. It is *beyond* talent, as it's nearly beyond human capacity. The *Gray Portrait* is your masterwork. Though you have, and often will, surpass it for glamour and allurement, and in every way, its terrifying authority you can never reproduce. Few could, or ever will."

"Yes," said Alice.

"It should be seen," Tirso said.

"Then have it."

"If the offered price–"

"Pay me nothing," said Alice, "I'll sign the proper papers. I gift it to the gallery willingly. That picture is already paid for."

Tirso rose to his feet. And she did so too.

Their eyes met in a look of gray stone.

"Paid. I understand it is," said Tirso. He saw she knew that *he* did, and that, for these instants, they were in an alternate eternity, and at one. "I'm certain, " Tirso said, "you have offered a very great and necessary service to both our cities. Perhaps to the world." He did not mean in her donation of the picture. And when she nodded, a quick, almost military movement, he could see she knew and accepted from him also, this.

Outside, as he walked towards the London Strand, where the sailor-story-teller Thames surged its muscular swarthy way inward and back, from and to the sea, the sun came out. Tirso remembered an afternoon the same, when he had left the country house in the hills north of Marcheval. Rifts of glowing light pierced the carnation sky. Objects were gilded topaz, the flying birds had wings of coral and gold. And here, the first warmth of a coming summer bloomed, and put its arm around his shoulders.

When she recollected him, which was very frequently, it was as if sunlight soaked through her heart and mind. She was instantly engulfed by a wash of happiness, hope, and peace.

This never lasted. Only for a moment, or the space of a swiftly-scrambled memory. Robert, the oasis in the savage desert of creation, her icon, her brother.

As a child she had loved him, despite the awful thing their father had once said, that Robert had *caused* their mother's death by being born. Even when she *heard* this said, when she was not yet six years old, and the appalling cries had stopped, and Sir William slumped drunk on a couch and ranted, sobbing; even then Alice had known that what had slain their mother was the wickedness of life's demons, never the child she presently was shown, and soon gently held. The child who grew as she grew, forwards into the boundless hot late springtime of youth, adolescence and young maturity.

Every recollection of Robert, even the first, was good.

She had seldom had to protect or avenge him. He was loved, (even their father loved him). Mathematically then the hate, when so rarely it came, had to strive to equal the love. It was, on both occasions, tremendous, in order to create a balance. Only two hates. Only twice. The pin she drove into the arm of the governess on that omnibus had been accidentally infected with something – unplanned, but entirely fatal. Alice had learned the woman died about three weeks later. From a wasp sting, it seemed. ("These wasps are so terrible this autumn.")

The portrait had been another pin, conceivably. The means to the sting of another wasp.

Now and then Alice dreamed of Robert, yet alive. They would eat ices or stroll to a theatre. They laughed and were glad.

No remembrance of him carried any pain.

Her rememberings, in fact, were the only times when really pain left her alone.

The snake that gnawed her heart. Nothing soothed it. Not that the agony was overwhelming. She could work through it very easily. She could *live* through it fairly easily. But it would not let go. The gnawing, the *sense* of the gnawing, eating her so slowly, so nimbly, so selectively away.

And sometimes too, at no specific hour, or due to no logical circumstance, she would catch again, like a distant yet very clear sound, that fragment of peculiar verse, whose author she had never traced. To go down and find the waters of forgetful night, and drink them in the dark and *un*remember, so nothing stayed but the sweet goodness of her recollections. Yet lodged deep as a sword inside her, the *hurt* of loss, separated from its focus, indefatigable, and so never to be escaped. And the poem was doggerel, apart from those last indelible and pitiless lines. Almost every day they came to her – on a stairway, at her easel, in the midst of conversation, hurrying to board a train. Like time moving on a clock, like a river tide. *Lethe leaves me to grieve, though I no longer know why.* Lethe, gray Lethe water, used to dip the brushes, translate the paint, from the tall jars, and the one small bottle afterwards tipped back into the restless river of Marcheval from which it came. Gray Lethe. That also, surreptitiously, bending to assess the highlight on a strand of hair, the crease of a sleeve, Alice had let fall, drop by tiny drop, into every thimble of tea, tulip bulb of wine, that Eugenie Valotif sampled as she sat for the *Portrait in Gray.*

About the Author

 Tanith Lee was born in North London (UK) in 1947. Because her parents were professional dancers (ballroom, Latin American) and had to live where the work was, she attended a number of truly terrible schools, and didn't learn to read – she is also dyslectic – until almost age 8. And then only because her father taught her. This opened the world of books to Lee, and by 9 she was writing. After much better education at a grammar school, Lee went on to work in a library. This was followed by various other jobs – shop assistant, waitress, clerk – plus a year at art college when she was 25-26. In 1974 this mosaic ended when DAW Books of America, under the leadership of Donald A Wollheim, bought and published Lee's *The Birthgrave*, and thereafter 26 of her novels and collections.

Since then Lee has written around 95 books, and over 300 short stories. 4 of her radio plays have been broadcast by the BBC; she also wrote 2 episodes (*Sarcophagus* and *Sand*) for the TV series *Blake's 7*. Some of her stories regularly get read on Radio 4 Extra.

Lee writes in many styles in and across many genres, including Horror, SF and Fantasy, Historical, Detective, Contemporary-Psychological, Children and Young Adult. Her preoccupation, though, is always people.

In 1992 she married the writer-artist-photographer John Kaiine, her companion since 1987. They live on the Sussex Weald, near the sea, in a house full of books and plants, with two black and white overlords called cats.

Also From Immanion Press

Ghosteria: Volume One: The Stories by Tanith Lee
ISBN 978-1-907737-61-9 IP0118 £10.99, $19.99

In this new collection, which contains most of the ghost stories of Tanith Lee – including 4 new tales original to this volume – Lee slips freely through the full gamut of Fantasy, SF, Horror, Historical, Parallel and Contemporary genres. The themes range, amongst others, with a lost love in early 20th Century New Zealand, a bullied child in 1970's India, into the underhill palace of a brooding magician in search of wonders, among the guests of a modern spiky wedding-breakfast, and beside a psychic, on a far planet whose damson skies are adrift with flying whales...

The moods conjured are dark, unnerving or plain nasty; or else sad, tender, kind and - now and then – outright crazy. Turn up the light. And don't look behind you.

Ghosteria: Volume Two: The Novel: Zircons May be Mistaken by Tanith Lee
ISBN 978-1-907737-63-3 IP0119 £9.99, $18.99

Sometimes when people die, it comes as a great shock. Even to them…

A group of the dead linger here, in the yellow dwelling on the hill – once a castle, then a stately home, now falling into ruin.

These ghosts drift and mingle, and brood on their lost lives. Death can be caused by so many things – war, pandemics, ordinary murder – even suicide or accident. Even time. But after death, surely, one could hope for peace? Not any more.

For with 2020 the New Apocalypse began. Civilisation crashed, and outside this ancient building things terrible, predatory, mindless and unkillable roam and bellow.

Now all the lights have gone out for good –
Where do you turn?

The Moonshawl by Storm Constantine
ISBN: 978-1-907737-62-6 IP041 £11.99, $20.99

Ysbryd drwg... the bad ghost. Hired by Wyva, the phylarch of the Wyvachi tribe, Ysobi goes to Gwyllion to create a spiritual system based upon local folklore, but he soon discovers some of that folklore is out of bounds, taboo... Secrets lurk in the soil of Gwyllion, and the old house Meadow Mynd, home of the Wyvachi leaders. The house and the land are haunted. The fields are soaked in blood and echo with the cries of those who were slaughtered there, almost a century ago. Old hatreds and a thirst for vengeance have been awoken by the approaching coming of age of Wvya's son, Myvyen. If the harling is to survive, Ysobi must lay the ghosts to rest and scour the tainted soil of malice. But the ysbryd drwg is strong, built of a century of resentment and evil thoughts. Is it too powerful, even for a scholarly hienama with Ysobi's experience and skill? 'The Moonshawl' is a standalone supernatural story, set in the world of Storm Constantine's groundbreaking, science fantasy Wraeththu mythos.

Para Kindred, edited by Storm Constantine & Wendy Darling
ISBN: 978-1-907737-60-2 IP0040 £11.99 $20.99

The androgynous and mysterious Wraeththu have risen to replace humanity upon a ravaged world. Based on the world created by Storm Constantine, these stories explore different, intriguing aspects of bizarre mutations and specialisations that have arisen, hidden within the developing Wraeththu tribes and throughout the corners of the world. Shape-shifters, semi-mythological beings, or hara who have evolved in other unexpected ways, Para Kindred expands the horizons of the Wraeththu world. Para Kindred features two new stories each by Storm Constantine and Wendy Darling, plus contributions from Martina Bellovičová, Ash Corvida, Nerine Dorman, Suzanne Gabriel, Fiona Lane, Maria J Leel, Daniela Ritter and E S Wynn.

Other Immanion Press Titles by Tanith Lee

The Colouring Book Series

Psychological tales and unsettling histories...

Greyglass 9781907737046 £10.99
The house... always growing, adding to itself, blooming, decaying, becoming reborn... But Susan doesn't live in the house of Catherine, her grandmother. When Catherine dies, no one mourns. The house is always changing. As if at last it must achieve some irresistible transformation. Frankly, there is something *uncanny* about the house. Isn't there.

To Indigo 9781907737213 £11.99
Don't talk to strangers. Don't even look at them. Novelist Roy Phipps leads an uneventful existence in the house inherited from his parents. His only aberration is the story he's been secretively writing for years of the mad poet Vilmos, a study of murder, angst and alchemic magic. Then one evening Roy meets Vilmos, face to face. As shadows close in on him, Roy understands he's now fighting for his own sanity. And probably his life.

L'Amber 9781907737251 £11.99
Jay has very little. Jilaine Best has everything. But even Jilane's perfect life is flawed, longing for the baby she's unable to conceive. She's willing to let another woman give birth for her. And so Jay confesses she is already pregnant with an unwanted child. Lies are so easy to tell, if you've had enough practice. Harder to change into truth. Spin your web. Watch it tangle. Now see what you've caught.

Killing Violets 9781907737367 £10.99
1934... Starving to death somewhere in Europe, Anna meets Raoul, who takes her to England and the dubious mansion of his arrogant and unsavoury relatives, the Basultes. Anna is a survivor. Both the aristocratic malignities, and the Hogarthian orgies of the servants,

can be accommodated, if they must. Anna has a past as savage and explicit as anything seen in the Basulte house.

Ivoria 9781907737404 £11.99
Nick Lewis certainly has no liking for his TV historian brother, Laurence. Aside from anything else Nick blames him for the death of their mother, the beautiful actress Claudia Martin. And so, is it possible the off-handedly childish trick played by Nick on Laurence really does cast some kind of curse? This is probably *not* a supernatural story. It might be less unsettling if it was.

Cruel Pink 9781907737497 £11.99
Emenie, a serial killer, lives alone. She can read omens and knows exactly her legitimate prey. Rod has a dreary life, working at an unrewarding job with something uneasy hanging over him. Is it the wardrobe? Klova is young, beautiful, living on benign handouts, in a Science Fantasy existence of sprints and liquid-silver...Until she meets the challenging Coal. Here, at the outskirts of this City they all call London, what the Hell is going on?

Turquoiselle 9781907737596 £11.99 *Also in Kindle Ebook*
Not much is what it seems. The job can be dull, but quite demanding. The work is lucrative, however. He can easily afford the costly wants of Donna, his partner. It's just that suddenly things are running less smoothly. This stuff with Donna... Various unusual tensions at work... the bizarre and threatening business over Silvia... In the end, maybe all you can rely on is yourself.

And In Ebook Through Kindle

Kill the Dead
Turquoiselle
Ghosteria Volume 1: The Stories
Ghosteria Volume 2: The Novel: Zircons May Be Mistaken

NewCon Press

http://newconpress.co.uk/

The very best in fantasy, science fiction, and horror

Colder Greyer Stones by **Tanith Lee**

Released to commemorate the author being honoured with a Lifetime Achievement Award at the 2013 World Fantasy Convention, this stunning collection of stories provides further evidence of why Tanith Lee is held in such high regard by fans and contemporaries alike. The book features twelve wonderful, rich-textured tales including the brand new novelette "The Frost Watcher" and five stories previously available only in the (sold out) signed limited edition "Cold Grey Stones".

Paperback: ISBN 978-1-907069-60-4   £9.99

Pelquin's Comet (The Dark Angels, Book One) by **Ian Whates**

Action-packed space opera from the author of *The Noise Within*.

In an age of expansion, the crew of the freetrader Pelquin's Comet race to claim a cache of alien technology they hope will make them rich. Pursued by the authorities and by corporate agents, they battle against enemies without and within, all under the watchful eye of an unwelcome passenger: an agent of the bank funding their expedition, who is far more than he seems and may represent the deadliest threat of all.

Hardback ISBN: 978-1-907069-77-2 £25.99
Paperback ISBN: 978-1-907069-78-9 £12.99